The Mistake

A person appeared in the distance, a vague shape, nothing more. Whoever it was seemed to tarry, as if waiting for her. Not normally apprehensive, she wondered who it could be. A friend perhaps? Her mind ran through the possibilities. As she came closer, she began to think that it was no one she knew, a stranger.

Young Witch Seeks True Love

Briana was not a very good witch. She had failed Spells 101, and she wasn't very good at Bi-location either. She could do a few tricks, but that didn't count for much. Even non-witches could sometimes do tricks. Her lack of skills was beginning to get her down.

From the Oasis

"If that is how it is, I will win your heart a little at a time. I will find sweet smelling night flowers and lay them next to your tent. I will find sparkling stones and leave them by your campfire. I will find the freshest fruits of the desert to lay at your side."

This book is a work of fiction. Names, characters, places and incidents are products of the author's imagination or are used fictitiously. Any resemblance to actual events or locales or persons, living or dead, is entirely coincidental.

Copyright © 2005 Tom Molnar

All rights reserved. No part of this book may be reproduced or transmitted without written permission from the author excepting quotation of brief passages (not poetry) for a review.

Printed in the United States of America.

ISBN 0-9766952-7-8

LOVE STROKES

Tom Molnar

Apple Valley Press

I would like to thank all those who have reviewed my fiction, and made welcome suggestions. They are too many to list. Thanks especially to Mary Jo Brunswick Shea and Andrew Molnar for their editing assistance.

Most importantly, I want to thank my wife, Kathleen, who provides me with the inspiration for romance.

Ten Stories...With Love

A Catch	1
Ancient Love Story	14
The Chainsaw Man	20
Jenny's Wish	35
Happily Ever After	38
Young Witch Seeks True Love	41
Strange Tale of Forgotten Love	63
The Mistake	69
From the Oasis	77
The Stranger Next Door	90

Bridestar 97

A Romantic Adventure Novel

Poetry Selections

Beach Time for Two	243
Used Life	246
Decision on High	249
Harvey and Emma	251
Don Pablo and Chiquita	253
She's Still There	258
A Small Reunion	259

Love Strokes
1

A Catch

Paul looked out the bedroom window at his estate. His manicured lawn led out to the wetlands where ducks and deer could frequently be seen. He had selected this site for his small mansion tucked far away in the suburbs. At only twenty-eight he was a very successful man. Son of migrant farmers, who eventually settled down, he had risen far above his heritage and had even changed his name. His given name, Pablo, wasn't good enough for him.

Paul loved the lifestyle, and he had no difficulty making executive decisions and directing others. He had a talent, a gift, for knowing what to do and when to do it. He was highly regarded, and as he was still single, sought after by women who could see a fine future with him. And yet, he was lonely. Successful as he was, he had not had success in love.

The phone rang. It was his mother. He had to revert to his little used Spanish to talk to her because, after all these years, she just couldn't get English. "*Ok, mama. Vendre. Si. Entiendo. Mis cumpleanos pequenos de hermana. Vengo.*" His mother was right, he had forgotten his younger sister's birthday. He would have to shower, eat, and run to the store to get something for her and then drive back into the city. He hated to have to rush on Sunday, his only day off.

Despite thick traffic, he made it on time. Everyone else was there. His parents, his brother Juan with his wife Belinda and their two children, and of course, his sister Rosa, along with a young man he didn't know. Judging by how he stayed near her, Paul guessed he was a boyfriend. Though family, Paul was not welcomed especially warmly, except by his mother who embraced him tightly and still called him Pablo. She would never change. He greeted the others and went to his young sister to personally wish her a happy birthday. She introduced him to Carlos who seemed personable enough, even shook his hand. Family together times were something that Paul had resigned himself to, for better or worse. He went to the fridge to get himself a beer.

Later that night, after fighting through a major traffic snarl on his way home, he thought a little about the day. His father still worked at his low paying factory job, his mom did some cleaning, and they all lived just above poverty. Yet they were basically happy. Of course, they would have liked nice things, but were satisfied with what they had. Maybe that was their problem, they were too satisfied. He thought about his sister, whom he noticed for the first time looked more like a woman than a girl. She was going to enter the local college in the fall while working part time. Good for her. Well, it was already time to think about tomorrow. Mondays were always busy.

The work week went by quickly, and now it was Saturday morning. He had a few things to do but finished early as he had a date that evening. She was a friend of a friend, and he had seen her, so she wouldn't qualify as a blind date, though he knew almost nothing about her except that she was pretty. Paul had had more than one bad experience with women which made him cautious. Still, he was looking forward to the evening.

He picked her up at her apartment, which was situated midway between the high and low rent districts. Her name was Maria; she looked and smelled lovely, all dressed in figure-revealing black. She had a good one. She sat straight in the car, not relaxed but attentive, as he drove them to the theater and they exchanged pleasantries. Her voice betrayed a Spanish accent, which he usually found unappealing, though not tonight. After parking, he held her hand as they crossed the lot. He noticed that she was not very tall, and would have been even shorter without the high heels. In a way he liked that, someone he could protect.

The movie was just so so, and afterward they went to dinner. He knew an intimate bistro with a comfortable, refined feel and good though limited menu. They sat in a booth and Angelo waited on them.

"Ah, ha, Mr. Martin. You are back! Good time no see."

Angelo was direct from Italy, and though he mixed up the language, he was always a ray of sunshine.

"Ah, Angelo, good to see you again. This is Maria. Maria, Angelo."

"So nice to meet you, Angelo," she said, extending her hand.

"Lovely. *Bella, bella*," he added, ceremoniously kissing her hand.

Maria lit up with a smile, Paul noted. It pleased him.

The evening went well. In fact, he had a very good time and Maria seemed to enjoy the night as well. He would definitely ask her out again.

After five dates they were passionate, or was it four? It didn't matter now what their evening plans were, because the time they spent together on his or her sofa made the night. He had already learned a lot about her, and she about him. She came from a poor family also but was able to get a scholarship to college and become an RN. It was obvious that she loved her family, no matter that none of them made it beyond high school and all worked menial jobs. She especially loved babies and would become excited whenever she talked about her brother's young children.

They had major differences. She was spontaneous, affectionate by nature, intuitive, and she truly cared about people. They were all qualities he recognized as positive, yet none that he possessed. In fact, he was rather the opposite. Calculating and rational, he withheld his feelings and thought about himself much more than anyone else, with the exception of her. It was surprising that they got on so well.

It was time for her to meet his parents. He had already met hers. He wasn't looking forward to having her meet his family, but she wanted to. He called his mother who sounded so happy when he told her about

Maria.

"*Venga el Domingo,*" she said. Sunday dinner it would be.

When they arrived he saw Juan's car. He had been hoping that Maria would only have to meet his parents. But they were all there, Rosa, his brother and his wife and children, and even Carlos. Opening the door, he ushered Maria in. Everyone looked their way and greeted them, and Maria went right over to his mom. They embraced, and Paul noticed that his mother was teary eyed afterwards. She was always so emotional. Maria didn't wait for introductions; she just started talking to Juan and Belinda as if she knew them and hadn't seen them for awhile. They introduced their children, Jose and Isabel, and after spending some time with them, Maria met and spoke with Paul's father. She said something to him that Paul didn't catch. Whatever it was, it seemed to melt the older man's typical reserve. Paul was surprised. In a matter of minutes she had charmed the house. When they sat down to dinner, none of the old, tired gripes and complaints were aired, and no one was belittled or chastised. Paul realized that he was smiling more than usual and that he even had some nice things to say to members of his family. When he and Maria were saying goodbye, he did so with a warmth that was new to him. Once inside the car, while still on the driveway, he turned to look at Maria. She was facing forward, smiling in a contented way.

"What are you smiling about" he asked.

Turning to him she replied, "You have a very nice family, Paul."

Maria loved them. She told him so the next day. She talked about each one and had already learned some things about his sister-in-law that even he didn't know.

That evening, Paul and Maria were going to the mall. He needed shirts and she wanted to go to a gift shop. After stopping for dessert they came back to his house and began to kiss. She closed her eyes and whispered "Pablo."

Paul immediately went rigid. Holding her back he said, "my name is Paul, not Pablo. Do you understand?"

The mood was broken. She met his eyes and without flinching said, "you were born Pablo. Pablo Martinez."

"Maria, I had my name changed over seven years ago. Please don't revert back to what I have left behind forever."

"It's a fine name, Paul," she said, careful not to say Pablo. "You come from good people. Sure, you can change your name to whatever you want, but you can't change your blood."

"I know that."

The evening died for them, and not long afterward she asked to be taken home. Late that night she tried to understand why he would be so adamant about his name. The only thing she could deduce is that he was ashamed of his own people. Maria loved her family and she appreciated the struggles they had made to achieve a better life. The whole incident made her think of Paul Martin in a different light.

Normally she called him at least once during the day. The next day she didn't. Paul realized that she was upset. He didn't call her either, thinking that in a day or two their little rift would blow over. When she didn't call the second day he became apprehensive, but thought he'd wait another day before calling. He was beginning to do some thinking about his life and about his name. Did a name really matter that much? When she didn't call the next day, he called her. It was in the evening, after work. The phone went immediately to her answering machine, and he hung up. He tried later and the same thing happened. Finally, after waiting another hour and still getting the answering machine, he left a message.

Love Strokes

"Hi, Maria!" He hesitated. "I'm sorry about our misunderstanding. Please don't think I don't like my family. I do. Very much. Let's talk. I'll be home tonight. Hope to hear from you soon."

Paul waited uneasily the rest of the night, playing computer games and watching television without having any interest in either. No call came. By the next day he realized he was getting frustrated. Memories of her kept breaking into his thoughts, and he felt he had to do something. He was beginning to worry that she might have been hurt in an accident or had a medical emergency. He was going through the phone book, trying to find her parents' number, when the phone rang.

"Hi."

"Maria! Are you alright? I've tried repeatedly to get hold of you."

"I'm fine Paul. You needn't worry. I've been out of town a couple days. I got your message that you want to talk."

"Yes. Yes. We need to talk. Tonight. Is that OK?"

"I have something I need to do tonight. It's important. I could meet you tomorrow."

"That's fine. I'll pick you up. We'll have supper. Is six o'clock alright?"

Maria said yes, but not in an encouraging way, he noted. It was as if she were doing it out of a sense of duty instead of looking forward to seeing him. Still, it was a start, one he could surely build on.

Throughout the day, he looked forward to meeting her. He wanted to make things right between them again. He left work, went straight to her apartment, and they drove to a nearby restaurant. After the five day absence she looked great to him, but he noted that she seemed sad. He sensed that maybe she had been crying. He treated her with tenderness, and they spoke casually; yet her mood didn't lighten. For a time they sat in silence on opposite sides of the table. Then he broached the topic of concern. She said, "Wait, Paul. Let's not talk about it here. At your house or mine."

They drove to his house where she sat down on one of the upholstered chairs, and he got her a glass of water. He sat down on the sofa, across from her.

"I'm sorry," Paul began, "about the misunderstanding. If it really means that much to you, you can call me Pablo, or Paco, or even Peter for all I care. I mean, what's a name?"

"It's not that, Paul," she said, her body leaning toward him. "It's me. Unlike you, I am always going to be who I am and that's

Love Strokes

Mexican. If you were German or Polish or something else I wouldn't care. But you aren't, and when you reject who you are, it could just as easily be me. And not just me, our people as well."

"Maria, I could never reject you."

"You say that, yet in a way you have turned away from your own family."

"Because I changed my name?"

"Why did you?"

"Maria, my parents were migrants, fruit pickers, before they finally settled to live in one place. As a kid I was there with them, out in the fields and orchards. It's something I wish I could forget. Furthermore, there's a lot of discrimination against migrants. You know that. Haven't you ever been called "wetback"? I'm not proud of my background, so I changed my name. Is that so bad?"

"So now you're filthy rich with the last name of Martin. I hope you're happy," she said, getting up to leave.

"Wait!" he yelled, going over to her and putting his arm around her. She shook in his grasp, not wanting to be held. "Maria!" he said loudly. "Please sit down. Let me tell you something."

"OK, what is it?" she replied sharply, taking a seat.

"Two things. I love my parents, despite what you might think. They don't want my money, but nevertheless, I help them out whenever I can. Secondly, I had to work very hard to get to where I am today. There was no one pulling strings for me."

Maria had been staring into space as he spoke, but now she looked directly into his eyes. She got up and sat down near him on the sofa. "Paul, I know you take pride in your work, and I believe you care about your parents. You think that you've come a long way from their migrant farming days. What you don't seem to realize is that they came a long way too."

"Yes, I know they are better off now than when they were picking fruit and vegetables."

"It's a lot more than that, Paul. They left the country that they grew up in to come to one with a language they didn't speak. They left all that was familiar in their lives to live among strangers and customs that were quite unknown. Like you, they did it for money and a chance for a better life. Don't you understand, Paul," she said, lifting her hands toward him. "It was they, not you, who were the real pioneers. It wasn't easy for them to completely change their lifestyle, but they had the courage to do it. It is only because your family and mine took that big step that you and I are where we are today. If anyone is self made, it's them, not us." She dropped her hands into her lap.

Paul was looking down as he listened to her talk, and he realized the truth in what she said. Raising his head, he turned to face her, his eyes glistening as they met hers. He took her hand in his, and then he embraced her, drawing her close, inhaling her fragrance. He kissed her gently. It wasn't enough. Hungrily his lips pressed hers, and after a brief resistance, she surrendered to his ardor. There was no need for words.

Approximately a year later, the wedding of Mr. and Mrs. Pedro Martinez took place in the Church of Our Lady of Guadalupe. The bride was radiant and the groom was unusually handsome. All the Martinezes and the Floreses and their friends and relatives filled the small church. The magic words were pronounced, rings were exchanged, and the happy couple walked down the aisle waving to their friends and relatives. Ten months later their first child arrived. "Made in America," someone said, as the family gathered to see for the first time, the Martinez' new baby boy.

Ancient Love Story

Donal was young, yet in some ways he was of the old school. His father was a respected shaman, and his mother had died in childbirth (not his). He grew up like the other youths in his clan, though having a shaman for a father did make a difference.

It was expected that he would follow in his father's footsteps, but Donal knew early on that it was not for him. The trances, the intonations, and the laying on of hands, didn't move him as they should have. It was not so much that he lacked faith, as that he looked at things from a different perspective. Why? He didn't know.

As the old ones started dying, he realized that he needed to do two things. He needed to settle into a job, and he needed to take a mate. His friends and most of his relatives were hunter-gatherers and he could always do the same. However, when the hunt was good, and therefore there was plenty to eat, he started hanging around old Tolpat, the flaker.

Tolpat's only son had died from a misdirected arrow so he was glad to have someone to sit with. Donal spent a lot of time with Tolpat, learning about different kinds of rock, their fault lines, and how to strike them with the right size and type of tool. He also learned about Tolpat's two daughters, one married and one not. Donal learned that it was the younger who was married, and when Tolpat introduced the other girl, Sarim, Donal saw why she was not taken. Though she was pretty, her left hand was scarred and limp, and she couldn't use it to grasp anything. Tolpat explained that she had been wounded by a tiger that was mistakenly thought to be dead. He said she had adapted so well she could do just about anything any other girl could do. Donal looked away. He felt sorry for her.

After several days of hunting, Donal returned to work with Tolpat. He liked the old man and he liked his trade. One day he even told him about his idea. Tolpat didn't laugh at him, even when he showed him some sketches he had made on flat rocks. Instead, Tolpat was encouraging and told him about the substances he often found in rocks that could add color to his sketches. Donal listened closely to Tolpat because he realized that no one else knew more about rocks.

Winter came, food grew scarcer and harder to find, and for a long time Donal had to be away on hunting expeditions. When spring came he knew that he was ready to take a mate, and he began an active search. Not satisfied with the few girls left in his own clan, he spent weeks away from home looking for what he could find in other clans. It was dangerous for him to do so, for youths often became angry if they thought an outsider wanted to take one of their beauties. That is, unless there was a surplus.

At the Huibogan clan things were quite different. There were so many marriageable girls there that the chief and his leaders decided to offer them freely to any eligible male who came along. Donal was able to look at nine young women, and he learned that he could sleep with whomever he chose.

The offer sounded great until he thought a moment and realized there would be a catch. The one he chose they would make his wife—forever. Knowing that, he looked at the girls more closely, and not just at their bodies. In the end he couldn't decide, and he didn't want to take a chance on getting stuck with someone who might be hard to live with. The clan leaders were not happy that he snubbed their daughters, and he needed to leave quickly before there was trouble. The incident made him think, and he decided to return home to his own people.

He had been away a long time, and already

there were some changes. His father was still hearty, but Tolpat, who was by now a friend, was not as well off. He confided to Donal that it was a sickness that had previously taken others of his family, and he was not hopeful of a recovery. He basically offered Donal his craft, which Donal could take over completely when he was gone. In addition, he offered him Sarim.

Donal was sad for Tolpat, but he knew it was the way of life. He thought about Sarim and remembered her smile. When he saw her again in person, he realized that despite her bad hand, she was a lot nicer to look at in the face than all the other girls he had seen. Then he went to talk to his father about it. His father spoke with him in the long way old men have of talking. He didn't encourage him, but then he didn't discourage him either. That was all Donal needed. He decided to take her.

He went back to Tolpat and gave him the news. Tolpat was happy, and Donal had never seen him smile so large. He even hugged him. Donal waited until Sarim came back from gathering, and he waited for Tolpat to give her the news. When she came out of the tent she walked toward him and smiled shyly at him. Donal waved his hand in acknowledgment. It was all he was expected to do, and yet it made him happy that she was agreeing. Not that it was really necessary.

Time passed quickly after that. Tolpat died before he could see his grandson, and then the other children came. Donal was happy with Sarim and found that she, unlike most of the women, almost never complained. Because she had the bad hand, he sometimes helped her when he wasn't too busy.

Four of their seven children lived past childhood, which meant he often had to both hunt and flake in order to provide for them. After a while, their children grew old enough to help and things became easier again. It was then that he had time to do some more of his sketching. He experimented with color, and one day when he had done a bison he thought was especially fine, he showed it to Sarim. He was surprised at her reaction. She really liked it. In fact, she held it in her hands next to her breast thinking it was a gift. Donal was pleased and he let her keep it. He could always make another.

The next winter was hard, much colder than any they could remember. The clan temporarily moved into a large cave until the weather improved. The cave life, while warmer, was damp and was hard on many in the clan. Some died, including Sarim. Donal had by now seen much sickness and death, but this time he was saddened. He had allowed himself to get too close, closer than was normal for a man and woman. When the weather broke, he, and everyone else, was glad to be outside again. Still, the cave had a hold on him, as that was where he had last seen Sarim.

One day, taking some supplies, he returned. Lighting two torches, he looked at the smooth surface on one side of the cave. He moved some large rocks closer to the wall so he could stand on them, and he wiped the surface with an old deerskin. Then he began to sketch. In his left hand he held the flat rock with the image she had liked so much. For days he worked on the project, sketching and then filling in the colors, until at last he was satisfied. It was fitting, he thought. It would be a lasting memorial to Sarim.

The Chainsaw Man

Sam stopped cutting for a moment. He heard his cell phone ringing. It was Veronica again, Roni, as he called her. He set down his saw.

"Yes, no problem, Roni. I can get over and do it. Not today though, I've got a big job on the south end of town. How about Wednesday, kind of late. I have another job over there and I can come over afterward."

He listened a bit to her then said, "Roni, you don't have to go to that much trouble."

"Sure, I'd like to. No, I don't have anything else planned. You realize I'll be kind of dirty, I mean working all day." He listened to her talk some more.

"Well, OK, and thanks. I'll bring an appetite."

He switched off and thought for a moment before going back to work.

That night, he thought more about the call. Veronica sure seemed to like him to come over. He'd cut so many trees and bushes at her house already; soon she'd run out of things for him to do. He smiled as he guessed at the real reason for the call. She must be interested in him. He thought about what he knew of her. She was a young widow, childless, who had cared for her husband for many months until cancer took him. That was over a year ago. Roni wasn't bad to look at, but Sam had pretty well decided that he'd rather not get involved with a woman again. Once was enough, especially in light of what happened. Sam didn't like to think about that although it changed his life forever. Sometimes, when it came back unbidden into his thoughts he was glad he had the chainsaw. He worked with a ferocity then, and anyone watching him might say, "damn, he's a hard worker." Sam preferred it that way. He didn't want anyone to know his secret.

Late in the afternoon he finished the job at the Hanley's, and after loading up his stuff, he drove his pickup over to Roni's. He saw her out on the deck as he rounded the corner, and she waved to him. He pulled into her driveway, slammed his ill-fitting truck door, and went around the side of the house.

"Hi, Sam. Nice to see you."

"Same here," he answered. Is that the overgrown shrub you want me to cut down?"

"Yes. Take it down right to the ground please. I want to plant something else there."

"OK. It won't take long."

"When you're done we'll have dinner. I'm making something I think you'll like."

" I appreciate it Roni, but it sure isn't necessary. I'll get my stuff from the truck."

In short order Sam had cut the big lilac tree to the ground and cut the large branches into firewood size pieces. He put his saws and the cut wood into his pickup. Dusting off his clothes, he rang the doorbell.

"You didn't have to ring," Roni said as she let him in. She had changed clothes and was wearing a simple attractive black dress and diamond earrings. He felt large and somewhat ungainly next to her trim shapeliness. He managed to say, "you look lovely, Roni."

"Thank you. You can wash your hands

Love Strokes

there," she pointed to the hallway bathroom, "and then we're ready to sit down to dinner."

It was a great dinner, and Sam ate until he was full. Afterwards, Roni asked if he'd like coffee and then brought out cherry pie. After coffee and two helpings of her delicious pie a la mode, Sam felt full and content. She turned on the television, and he sat back comfortably on her sofa while she sat next to him. They talked. She was easy to talk to; he found she wanted to know more about him, and he was interested in knowing more about her. However, his reserve held him back, and he temporized, not willing to reveal too much. He felt a sadness when he got up to leave, because he realized that despite her upbeat manner, at heart she was lonely, and it was a feeling he knew a lot about. Still, he was not ready to open up to her because he was afraid of what she would think if she knew the truth. He said goodbye and thanked her for the fine dinner.

He couldn't get her off his mind. Two days later he called her up and asked her out. They went to a play, a local production of a musical. The acting wasn't anything to write home about, but the music was well done. Many in the cast had excellent voices. Afterward, they went for dessert and talked about the play. Then he took her home. This time he kissed her, and she kissed him back. It had been a long time since anyone had kissed him.

The next day he called her, and they talked awhile on the phone. He was still somewhat leery about letting her know more about him, but he could see the way things were going he was going to have to tell her. He invited her to go with him Sunday to the mountains, about an hour and a half drive. He suggested that they could hike up a mountain trail leading to a lake where they could picnic and swim. She said she usually went to church on Sunday, but could go Saturday evening instead. She invited him to go with her. Sam thought about it briefly. He sometimes went to church, different ones, as he didn't really want to become regular where people might get to know him. "OK," he said at last.

"Great," she said. "Come by for me at quarter till five."

The service was not too different from others he had gone to, but all during it he felt both pride and warmth at having a lovely woman at his side. He even sang with her, and he hadn't sung in church since he was a kid. He had to admit, it was kind of special.

Love Strokes

25

The next day they got off to an early start. Roni had coffee and rolls ready; they ate breakfast together and then filled their backpacks with lunch, water, towels and swimwear. Sam took the wheel, put on some music, and drove toward the hills. It was a fine September day, one of the last warm days of the year before fall. He was glad Roni was adventurous enough to go with him.

They chatted as they drove and in no time reached the parking area, put on their backpacks, and headed up the trail. Sam knew the way very well, as it was one of his favorite spots. He had come here several times, usually in colder weather when his business slowed down. He started off at an easy pace, in consideration for Roni, until she asked him if he would like to go faster. He then proceeded at his normal speedier pace and saw that she had no trouble at all keeping up. "You're a good hiker, Roni," he said.

"Thanks. I like to think that the walking and jogging I do keep me fit for days like today." She was quiet a moment. "You said you were divorced eight years ago but never said much about it. Do you have any children?"

"Yes, one, a girl. Her name is Mia."

"Such a pretty name. Do you see her much?"

"No, unfortunately I don't see her at all, though I'd love to."

"Why don't you?"

"It's a long story, Roni. I'd rather not talk about it now."

"OK," she replied.

"I'll tell you about it sometime, just not today."

They continued their ascent and began talking about other things. Sam was glad she didn't press him; he felt so uncomfortable when people did that. In fairness to her, however, he knew that soon he would have to tell her about his life.

At last they reached the top and saw the lake. People were already sunbathing on the big boulders on one side or enjoying the water and the small beach on the other. They decided to swim first before eating lunch. Roni had expected that there would be a place to get into her swimsuit, but since there wasn't, they separated and changed behind bushes. When they returned to the beach they spread the large towel out on the sand. Then, without waiting for him, she ran out into the water and turned back to look at him. He strode out to join her in the water. She was standing up to her waist in water, and he admired how pretty she looked. She came closer, and he thought she was going to embrace him, but instead she pushed him, almost knocking him over, and then swam toward deeper water. The chase was on. Sam

Love Strokes

started swimming toward her, but soon realized he was making almost no headway. The girl was an athlete! He redoubled his effort and finally managed to catch up to her. By this time they were both in deep water and breathing hard. She was smiling at him, her dark wet hair creating a lovely frame for her charming face. They treaded water next to each other while they caught their breath.

"Jeez, Roni, you surprise me. You sure are in great shape for a school teacher."

"Thanks," she answered. "I assume you're talking about my swimming."

"That too," he was quick enough to respond, as he reached to hold her around the waist. "I don't know about you, but I'm about ready for that lunch you packed."

"You're just a big hungry boy," she said impishly. Let's go for it. First one back serves the other."

"That's a challenge. On your mark, get set, go."

It had been a wonderful day, Sam reflected when he returned to his house that evening. He was finding things out about Roni that he didn't know, and the more he learned, the more he liked her. He knew himself, and he knew that he was already falling hard for her. It was time she knew more about him before he got in any deeper. He took courage and called her. "Sorry about calling so late. I had a wonderful time today, and I'd like to see you tomorrow after work if you're free. I'd like to talk to you."

"Sure, Sam. Tomorrow's fine. I'll make supper for us."

"Don't bother. We can eat out to save you the trouble."

"It's no trouble, Sam. Come over when you're done with your work."

"OK. Thanks." He switched off and then stared at his phone. Already, he was getting nervous.

Morning came and Sam had another big job to do. He got to the site a little earlier than usual, and studied what needed to be done so he could tackle it in the most efficient way. He almost never started the actual cutting before eight a.m. in consideration of the neighbors. The day passed fairly quickly, and at five o'clock he was packing his things in the truck. His customers today wanted the wood for their fireplace, so he didn't have to haul it. He used their bathroom to clean up a little, and then he was in his truck, heading to Roni's. He didn't know exactly what to say first.

Love Strokes

When he arrived at her house, she heard him and stepped out onto her front porch. He waved hello as he approached and took a good look at her. He wanted to be able to remember her in that way, friendly, casual, pretty, in case he never saw her again. He realized he was very tense. She welcomed him with a hug and then got him a beer while she finished getting the meal ready. At supper they chatted about their day and afterward went to the living room and sat down together on the sofa.

Sam got up his courage and began, "Roni, we were talking about my daughter Mia yesterday. There's a big reason why I don't see her. I'm not allowed to."

"What do you mean, Sam?"

He took a deep breath. "I've been reluctant to tell you this, but I've got a record. That's why I can't see my daughter."

"I'm so sorry for you, Sam."

"Yes, it tears me up Roni. Sometimes I go to the mall and eat something at the Food Court. When I see a girl about my daughter's age, I just look at her, wishing I could give my daughter a big hug. After all these years I've never gotten over missing her."

"That's sad. John and I couldn't have children though we both wanted them. We started trying to adopt. Then he got cancer."

30

"I'm sorry."

"Yes, it was hard," she said simply, leaving much unsaid.

Sam reached for her hand and held it between his as they turned toward each other. He released it as he continued his story. "I spent six years in prison, Roni. He looked at her and decided to just blurt it out. "It was for murder."

"Sam! You don't mean it!"

" I'm afraid so, Roni."

"Sam, I can hardly believe this. You seem so gentle and considerate."

"There were special circumstances. Kelli and I had only been married for eighteen months. I was working for an equipment rental company, and one day I got off early and came home to find my wife in bed with another man. I grabbed the nearest thing I could find, a baseball bat. I didn't want to kill him. When he ducked, the bat hit his head. He died shortly afterwards in the hospital." Sam had not looked at Roni while he spoke. He turned to face her, and couldn't read her expression. He continued. "I got out early for good time and because of the circumstances. I quickly found out that people don't forgive and don't forget. I served my time but couldn't get any kind of decent job. Finally, I moved from Cincinnati

Love Strokes

31

and started this saw job. I don't do bad with the cutting and selling firewood, but no one would hire me on a regular job."

"Didn't you get a lawyer?"

"Well, I got one, but not having had any criminal experience, I didn't know who was good. It might not have made a difference anyway."

"Did they believe you when you told them it was an accident?"

"Oh, I don't know, Roni. You know I'm just an ordinary guy. I was enraged at the time of the incident and afterward was mad and heartbroken about Kelli being unfaithful. Throughout the whole arraignment and trial and sentencing I wasn't thinking very clearly. My whole world had suddenly been turned upside down."

"They wouldn't let you see your own daughter after you got out?"

"No. Kelli divorced me eight months after I was in prison. Then she got an injunction forbidding me from any contact with my daughter. I can be arrested if I drive past my old house!" He looked into Roni's eyes searching not for pity, but for acceptance.

"Sam, this is a lot to take in. I don't know what to say."

Sam could feel anger beginning to boil up inside him. The few people he had told had reacted negatively. He couldn't read Roni right now and that wasn't good. He stood up, and when she continued to sit there he said, "I'll be going now." She still didn't get up and he walked to the door and let himself out. Tears began streaming down his cheeks as he drove away.

As days went by with no call from Roni, he realized that it was probably over. And yet, he couldn't forget about her. He tried to fill his life by watching television, playing video games, and renting movies, but the void was still there. In a way he felt he had made a mistake in letting himself become involved again with a woman. Yet, he couldn't dismiss her entirely. It was too bad that even she couldn't forget the past. The days passed into weeks. Then, two weeks to the day, she called.

"Sam, are you OK? Why haven't you called me?"

At first he didn't know what to say without saying volumes. Finally, he said, "I didn't know if you wanted to see me."

"Of course I do. Badly."

"Me too. Can I come over now?"

"Yes. The sooner the better."

Love Strokes
33

Sam didn't waste any time. A quick wash of his face and hands, some Listerine, and he was on his way. As he rounded the corner to her house, he saw that she had left the porch light on. Pulling into her driveway, he momentarily saw something dark to his left. He opened his squeaky pickup door, and stepped out. Something brushed him and he turned around. It was Roni.

"Roni!

"Thanks for coming right over, Sam. I missed you so much."

He took her in his arms and they kissed. "I missed you too."

"Come on inside."

He took her hand and they walked in together.

"I'm sorry, Sam," she said once they were in the house.

"What do you mean?" he asked.

"I didn't know what to think when you told me everything. I'm sorry," she said again.

Sam could see that tears were welling up in her eyes.

"Let's sit down. We can talk. Roni, you don't have to be sorry."

"Yes I do, Sam. I didn't want to be like those other people. All those people who never could forget your past. I didn't want to be like them, and yet I was. I was afraid, Sam. I guess I'm not really very strong."

"It's OK, Roni," he said, taking her in his arms.

"I just kept thinking of it, running it over and over in my mind both day and night. I did a lot of crying, and I wanted to see you again. Finally I couldn't stand myself anymore. Who was I passing judgment on you, maybe throwing away a chance for happiness." She raised her head to look fully into his eyes.

He didn't say anything, just looked into her eyes that were so full of concern. Then he smiled, a big wide smile as he continued to look at her.

"What's funny?" she asked, perplexed.

"You are," he answered, "falling for a guy like me."

"Maybe so, but I like it," she said snuggling closer.

Jenny's Wish

Jenny closed the cover of the book, turned off the lamp, and cried. It was so beautiful. Tears still flowed down her cheeks. She might have sobbed as well, but in consideration of her husband sleeping next to her she didn't. She looked at him, his steady pattern of breathing leaving no doubt that he was dead to the world. Too bad, she thought. She wished he were awake and in tune to how she felt. Then he would have been up, loving her passionately, and she would have been fulfilled, again. No such luck tonight. She turned off the little lamp next to the bed, pulled the sheet over her, and eased her body down so that she lay flat on her back. Then carefully, so as not to wake him, she moved next to her husband and turning, held onto his body.

He stirred. Was he awakening? She waited, hoping it was so. No, just one of those sleep movements. Still, she was happy. Nick was a good guy, and the longer she was married to him the more she realized it. Certainly not a romantic, more of a rational type, he fit her. He didn't see all the things she saw in how people relate, but he understood other things, other necessary things that eluded her. Anyone would say they made a good pair. She snuggled a little closer to him.

He moved again. Was he waking? "Nick," she said softly.

"Yes?" he answered in a voice heavy with sleep.

"Nothing," she answered, not wanting to take him from his slumber.

"What is it?" he asked, still half asleep.

"It's nothing. Nick, I love you."

"I love you too, honey."

It was music to her ears. Whenever he said that. Especially now, after the romantic novel. "Nick, I love you so much." She needed to say that.

He roused from his slumber and sat up in

Love Strokes

bed and looked at her by the nightlight.

"Honey, is something wrong?"

"No, not at all. It's just that sometimes I realize how much I love you, and I just feel it."

He smiled. Then he got up and went into the bathroom. When he came back he gathered her in his arms.

It was all she could have hoped for, and she smiled, misty eyed, knowing, feeling, how she was loved.

Happily Ever After

God, she loved him. Waltzing down the aisle after the ceremony, Amy felt a wholeness holding the hand of her friend and lover. They would be together, forever. Happily ever after. Of course she knew Joe had his faults, and she knew she did too, but love would take care of those things. Her smile was radiant.

Time passed. Day to day life went on, and she learned some things along the way. She was still in love; nevertheless there were ups and downs varying from outright anger to sweet ecstasy. They were living life together, *their* way. It wasn't perfect but it was very good.

Children came, beautiful little ones, fashioned in the likeness of him and her. How wonderful they were! Their love was increased.

The cares of life swept in on them. A sick child, a job that didn't last, money problems, misunderstandings, lack of time, lack of sleep. It was far from idyllic. Yet somehow they managed; and when they weren't fighting, they were loving. They remained true to each other.

The children grew up, left home, married, and soon had children of their own. Life was passing so fast. Grandma and grandpa looked on with delight at the new life and gathered the young ones into their arms. They took them to the playground, shopping, fishing, and told them bedtime stories, and at Christmas time they showered them with gifts. And then, the grandchildren grew up too.

Gradually, they got old. Grandpa began walking with a limp, and grandma's sharp memory started to fade. "Pa," as the grandkids called him, was the first to go. She wanted to go too, to be with him. She and her children cried together and she realized that they were all going to miss him very much. She needed to be strong. She would help them carry on. She knelt down again by her husband in the casket and said a prayer to him. "Wait a little longer, and I'll be with you. This time, it really will be 'happily ever after.'" She stood up and looked with pride at her younger son, who had remained there with her. "Son, I think it's time we should go." He took her hand and slowly they walked out of the room.

Young Witch Seeks True Love

Briana was not a very good witch. She had failed Spells 101 and she wasn't very good at Bi-location either. She could do a few tricks, but that didn't count for much. Even non-witches could sometimes do tricks. Her lack of skills was beginning to get her down.

She wasn't bad looking for a witch. No obvious deformities that stood out. Certainly, no one would call her beautiful. Yet, there was definitely something you could see about her if you looked hard enough. Cuteness? Yes, that was it. It appeared in her pert smile, which she was careful not to display very often.

What was she going to do? It just seemed like her life was going nowhere. All her friends chatted excitedly about the various bewitching specialties they were entering. Briana just hoped that she would be able to graduate. She had to admit that her future didn't look too bright.

Maybe that's what got her thinking about the unthinkable—young men. Had she been a more powerful witch, like her friends, she wouldn't need to. As it was, she felt vulnerable, and the idea of having a boyfriend didn't seem too bad. In fact, it was appealing. She didn't know how to go about it, but she made her mind up then and there that she wanted to find one. Of course, she would have to keep it a secret from the others. She would be laughed out of the house if they found out. Nevertheless, just the thought gave her a feeling of hope, and when she considered it she felt that maybe she could be good for a young man. She could do a little magic occasionally for his entertainment, and they could share ordinary human things. She wouldn't ask for much.

The job of becoming a practicing witch was not easy, and it didn't allow very much time for other pursuits. At her very next opportunity, however, Briana went to the shopping mall where she hoped to find out something about boy-girl relationships. She was such a complete novice that she was afraid she wouldn't know how to act.

After walking around the mall for over an hour, she felt better. Many of the couples seemed happy in each other's company, and some held hands. She didn't see anything that she would have any trouble doing herself. Toward the end of that time, as the mall was closing, she noticed a young man who sat alone on a bench as if he was waiting for someone. He was slender, wore a short brown coat and had blond hair. What struck Briana about him, as she passed by him for the third time, was his earnestness. It was as if he were waiting for someone, someone he really didn't think would come. Her heart tugged a little when she looked at his wan face. If she had been more courageous, she would have sat down next to him and said something. He definitely looked like he could use some cheering up.

She thought about him often in the next few days. She decided that she was going to go back to the mall to try to find him. This time she would be prepared. She began working hard on spells and thought that she could at least do a simple spell to make him notice her. Next, she tried divination. Unfortunately, she had never been very good at that either. Peering into her crystal ball, she just couldn't make out when exactly he would be at the mall. The best she could narrow it down to was either Friday or Saturday night. She bit her lip in her nervousness and her ineptitude, and resolved that she would go there both nights if necessary.

  Now, what to wear? She threw her hands up in frustration. What do decent young men like? She was so inexperienced! She knew, of course, what wicked boys liked. Her witches' training had made that clear. She preferred a nicer sort, however, though she might take a little bad with the good. She looked hard at her limited wardrobe. Finally, she picked out something she hoped would be appealing.

  Friday night. Briana's heart palpitated as she dressed. She looked at herself in the mirror and was generally satisfied. Her honey-blond hair gleamed. There was no question, she wouldn't even try to take the broom. She was going to drive like a proper girl. If he should want to take her home, she could always get the car later.

  She felt excited as she entered the mall. Her exhilaration quickly dimmed as she looked around and didn't see him. She walked slowly, peering into all the stores, until she began to grow tired from so much concentrated looking. She sat down on a bench and began to feel quite lonely. So many couples strolling together having a good time, and here she was, dressed up and alone. In her sadness, her eyes drooped and she wondered what was she doing, a witch, looking for a man. It wasn't natural. She didn't even notice when someone sat down at the other end of the bench. When she looked up, she couldn't believe her eyes. It was him.

She lowered her head a little, and trying not to be too obvious, she studied him. He was nice looking. Clean, with sensitive mouth and eyes, yet virile too. Suddenly his eyes glanced over to her. She turned quickly away, and then, realizing that she had been discovered, turned back and smiled. He smiled too—a warm smile that made her feel good. "What's your name?" he asked.

She took a deep breath and replied, "Briana."

The evening was wonderful. When she thought about it, it wasn't that they did anything special. They had just stayed in the mall, looked at different things there, and talked. He bought her an ice cream, they laughed about everyday things, and that was it. When the mall closed they parted without a kiss. She wondered about that. Did he like her? She sure liked him. At the end he did get her telephone number and said he would call. She was glad she had gotten a cell phone. She couldn't imagine what he'd do if he called the house and they answered with their usual "Witches brew."

Days passed without a call. Briana grew more and more anxious. She hoped he hadn't found out about her background. Finally, the phone rang and it was him. Fortunately she was outside where she could talk without others listening. She wanted to talk to him, a lot. However, he seemed rushed. He asked if she would like to go to the show with him, and if she was free Saturday night. "Yes, yes," she twice answered affirmatively.

"O.K. I'm looking forward to seeing you again. Oh, I can pick you up at your house. Where do you live?"

Briana hesitated. She didn't want him to come to there, where he might see the other witches. "Nick, I need to get something at Wal-Mart which is nearby. Can you just pick me up there?"

"Sure. Seven thirty O.K.?

"Yes. I'll wait for you right outside the door.

"Good. See you then."

As he hung up, Briana sighed. She would have to tell him something, if not the whole truth, sooner or later. Later seemed better right now.

At the Movie Ten they reviewed the billings and soon realized that there wasn't a lot to choose from, after they nixed *Chainsaw Massacre III*, *Little Puff's Boat Trip*, *Harry and Denise*, and *Killer Bees*. The only two left worth seeing were *Tiger's Revenge*, and *Pandemonium*. They settled on *Tiger's Revenge*, which at least sounded exciting.

It was a thriller, featuring a streak of saber tooth tigers that had been resurrected through DNA synthesis in an island laboratory. Briana scrunched in her seat, and sometimes covered her eyes as the tigers pounced on, slashed, and disemboweled their hapless victims. Nick put his arm around her, and that made it bearable.

Afterwards, they stopped for dessert, and then he drove toward her house. Briana hoped when they arrived that none of her sisters would be around. He walked her to the door, and in the dim porch light he took her in his arms and kissed her. She didn't hold back, but returned his kiss with feeling. When he said goodnight, his voice seemed different, deeper. She waved goodbye as he drove off, and was smiling as she went inside.

Briana saw a lot of Nick in the coming weeks, and she began to feel emotions that she had never before experienced. In some ways, she was confused, and she felt a strong need to talk to someone about how she felt. She wished she had a good friend who was not a witch, who might know something about it. She wondered. Who did she know that she could talk to? Then she remembered someone. "Ah, Jenny," she said aloud.

Jennifer had dropped out of witches school over a year ago. She just didn't have it in her. Yet, she was nice, and they had been friends. She tried to think of her last name. It was an unusual name, she remembered. Jenny, Jenny. . . Jenny Fuddlerucker. That was it. She went to the phone book and looked it up. When she tried calling, a recording answered and gave her another number. Apparently she had moved. On the second try she reached her.

"Hi, Jenny. This is Briana. Remember me?"

"Of course, Briana," came the friendly, reassuring reply.

Love Strokes

"I hope I didn't call at a bad time."

"No, no. This is a good time. It's funny you should call, because I've recently had you on my mind."

"Really. That *is* a coincidence."

They talked awhile longer and then Briana said, "Jenny, I'm just bursting to tell you about a person I've met."

"A man?"

"Yes. How did you know?"

"Intuition. Say, why don't we meet somewhere, and catch up on everything."

Later that evening, at Ebson's café, the two shared dessert and soft drinks at a small round table. Briana was talking. "I like him a lot, but what's going to happen when he finds out I'm a witch?

"A former witch," Jenny corrected. "Or, at least a non practicing witch. Right? You don't do that stuff anymore, do you?"

"Not really. Oh, maybe just a little."

"I think I know what you mean. Little tricks to make things better, but nothing they could say, "Look! She's got supernatural powers!"

"Yes, that's it. Like I did a spell so Nick would notice me when we first met."

"I wouldn't worry about it so much. If he really likes you, it won't matter. Besides, men like a little magic."

"Does Frank?"

Jenny winked and said, "He certainly does."

Briana felt a lot better after talking with her friend. Not that there weren't some things she still didn't understand. Having grown up with girls, she was struck by the difference in their thinking and Nick's. His responses often surprised her. She noticed, as well, his complete lack of interest in some topics and his passion for others. He really was unpredictable. It was almost as if he were a different species. She resolved to try to understand him better.

Time passed. Nick and Briana continued dating, and now she even let him pick her up at the house. Her friends thought she was wacko, but for the most part, they weren't mean or unfriendly to her. Nick had met some of them, and he thought *they* were unusual. Nevertheless, he was always cordial, and after awhile they responded in kind and actually seemed to like him. When Nick picked her up on this particular night, he said something that implied that tonight would be special. Briana didn't need any witches' power to divine what it was. She felt that their relationship was deepening, and yet Nick still hadn't appeared to recognize her background. She regretted that she was going to have to tell him, and she was afraid of what he might say or do. She hoped that they could continue to see each other. With these thoughts in mind, it was with some trepidation that she stepped into his car that evening.

"Where are we going," she asked, as casually as she could.

"Minerva's, if that's OK with you.

"Oh, yes, that sounds like fun."

Minerva's was popular with old and young alike. No one would call it fancy, though they might call it unique. On one side was a nice restaurant where you could order Greek, as well as American food. On the other side, or through two doors in the middle, was a lounge with a large oval bar and a dance floor to one side of it. Most of the young crowd just went to the lounge, for drinking and dancing. Tonight Nick and Briana were going to both.

They had finished their meal and had ordered dessert, when Nick placed a small package near her plate.

"What is it?" she asked.

"Open it and see."

She removed the ribbon, with unsteady hands, then found the scotch tape that secured the gold wrapping paper. Removing that, she found a small green box. Nervously she opened the box and gazed down at an exquisite diamond centered in a white gold ring. She looked up at Nick who reached across the table to hold her hands in his.

"Try it on," he suggested.

She sensed deep tenderness in his voice, and she carefully laced the ring on her finger. "Nick, it's so beautiful."

"Not nearly so beautiful as your eyes. Briana, will you marry me?"

"Yes, Nick, yes," she said.

Despite her plans, Briana found she was unable to say anything to Nick about her past. The evening was too beautiful to spoil. She proudly glanced at her ring from time to time as she danced in his arms. Nick was more charming than ever. She would be glad, so glad, to have him be hers for always. How handsome he was! She felt so happy she could cry. When he took her home she was still in seventh heaven, helped, no doubt, by three glasses of wine, and even

Love Strokes

when she slept, beautiful dreams danced through her head.

When she awakened, the first thing she looked at was the diamond still perched on her ring finger. Suddenly it hit her. Nick still didn't know about her association with witchcraft. She wondered, as she went through the day, just how she would tell him. When she thought he would be back from work she called him. "Nick, I've got to talk to you."

"You sound so serious. You're not going to give me back the ring are you?"

"Oh, no! That's not it at all. I just need to talk to you."

"OK. Why don't you come right over. By the time you get here I'll have showered, and we can get something to eat."

"OK. I'll be right there."

She knocked on his apartment door and stepped inside. Nick was still in the shower so she looked over his place. She had only been there once before, and then only briefly. It was a man's place for sure, with comfortable furniture and natural, refreshing smells.

"Hi," said Nick, stepping out of the shower with a towel around his waist. "You made it here fast."

"Too fast, I see. I'll start fixing

something in the kitchen while you get dressed."

Nick soon returned from the bedroom, and coming into the kitchen he kissed her. "So what is it that's so important you need to tell me right away?"

"Better sit down, Nick," she began. Nick rolled his eyes and took a seat.

"Nick, there's something about me that you should know."

"This is getting interesting."

"Really, I'm serious. This is hard for me to say." She put the plates down and went over to sit near him on the couch. "Nick, I don't know any other way to tell you." She hesitated. "I'm a witch," she said, bowing her head in shame.

Sensing her feelings, Nick moved over and put his arm around her. "What do you mean? What did you do?" he asked.

She looked up at him through teary eyes. "It's not what I did, it's what I am. You see, I was raised as a witch, and I've been in a school for witches."

"Wait. I really don't know what you are saying. To me you're special. I've never thought of you in any other way."

"I know that, and I'm glad. Still, you should know the truth, especially if I'm going to wear your ring."

"Briana, do you want to know the truth? The truth is, I don't believe in witches."

"What? What did you say?" she answered, taken aback.

"I don't believe in witches."

Suddenly, all of Briana's training flashed before her, and she thought of all the skills of her witch friends. All she could say in response was, "I can't believe you're telling me this, Nick."

Nick leaned toward her, and took her in his arms. "Even if you are a witch, I still love you."

Briana was thinking about what he said before. She had never considered that anyone would simply not believe in witches. Finally she said, " I should turn you into a frog." Nick laughed loudly, his head pitching backward while he kept his hold around her waist. Briana turned to look at him, and she smiled. Again, he had completely surprised her. She snuggled in his arms.

As far as Briana was concerned, everything was settled. Nick had accepted her, and even if he didn't really believe she was a witch, she could always say, "I told you so." Actually, she was anxious to get married, so that she could live happily ever after with her friend and lover. Nick, however, had other plans. Whereas Briana just wanted to do it, Nick wanted to do it right. He drove her to a new subdivision at a spot where a grassy area overlooked a meadow. "What do you think of this location," he asked.

"It's nice. What a view!"

"I'd like to buy a lot here and build on it. I figure that doing much of the work myself in my spare time, it would be ready for us to move into in a year."

"You could do that?"

" Yes. I've learned as much as I can on the job about building homes, and I've helped friends with theirs. I'm ready to do one for us. You could help with the planning. We could do it together."

"That's exciting. Living anywhere with you would be wonderful, but a new house would be awesome. I'm sure it would be a tremendous amount of work, though. Are you sure you want to do this?"

"Yes. You inspire me to do great things."

"OK. If that's what you want. Just letting you know, I'd be happy living with you just about anywhere."

Nick pulled her close and looked at her in that tender way that always melted her heart. "I know that, darling. That's why you're going to have the best."

With a year to wait for the wedding, Briana decided that she also should do something constructive. After thinking of alternatives, she settled on becoming a beautician. She already helped her friends at the house with their zany hair styles, and once trained she could quickly have a following. With the size of the house that Nick was talking about, she could even work from home.

At last, the long year passed, and it was the night before the wedding. The witch house was in a frenzy. All twenty-seven had been invited, as Briana didn't know how to turn anyone down. Many of them had never been to a wedding, and she was afraid they wouldn't know how to act. Briana had talked to her friends, asking, pleading, that they be on their good behavior, but she was still worried. Oh, how she wished that it was all over with and that she could just be alone with Nick. Well, she made her mind up to make the best of it, regardless of how it all came off. She just hoped that none of the witches did anything really wicked.

The house reeked with the odors of burning candles, various incenses, and the cauldrons steaming with magical ingredients. The witches were doing everything they could to insure her a rapturous transition to this new lifestyle, and they were preparing talismans to protect her from calamities. Briana was edgy on the evening of her wedding, and she was careful not to violate any of the taboos related to the occasion. Besides that, she was also asking for heavenly assistance, in the simple way Nick taught her. Even with that, she would have been petrified at the thought of permanent commitment, had it been with anyone else but him.

Somehow, she finally fell asleep, and in the morning she felt refreshed. Ah, this was the day! With almost all the preparatory things done, she looked forward to her wedding. In the light of day, she was practical enough to realize that, even if things didn't come off as planned, the result would still be the same—she would be married to Nick.

Love Strokes

To her surprise, the wedding ceremony went almost without a hitch. The reception, however, was another story. As they entered the hall, to the announcement, "And now, for the first time, introducing Mr. and Mrs. Nick Penman," the stiletto of her high heel broke, and as the crowd turned toward them, she stumbled forward, managing somehow to keep her balance. It would have been better if she had fallen down. Nick rushed to assist, and helped her to stand up straight. She tried walking forward with him, but with one shoe flat, and the other high, she walked like she was drunk. Finally, discarding both shoes, she and Nick made their way to the head table.

Then the lights went out. The manager of the establishment quickly came and explained that they had found a dead raccoon in back beneath the power line, and that the electric service company had been notified. He was sorry. Of course, there was no working microphone, so Janis, one of Briana's bridesmaids, spoke up and announced that she and her friends would provide lighting until service was restored. With that, all twenty-seven of the witches gathered in the open area in front of the head table.

The rest of the guests became quiet, wondering what they were going to do. In the dim light of the lone emergency lamp, the witches formed a circle. They began whispering, then humming, then chanting. Something started glowing in their midst, a translucent ball of crimson that began rising from the floor. The witches stood with their arms toward it, urging it to rise higher. At the same time, swirling mists emanated from the region of the glowing ball, and spread from the circle toward the guests. The vapor was cold and damp, and to get away from it, people started heading toward the exits.

"Wait," the disc jockey cried out. "They're getting the power turned back on!"

Nick turned to Briana. "Honey, we're losing our guests."

Briana stood up and shouted, "Stop! Janis, Raquel, Melissa. Everybody. You've got to stop it! You're scaring them."

The witches turned to look at her. The spell was broken and the crimson ball gradually faded. The guests, most of whom had stayed near the exit doors to see what would happen, started returning to their tables. Some carried candles provided by management. Finally, power was restored, and the reception commenced.

After the comedic start, it turned out to be a wonderful affair. For once in her life Briana felt beautiful, and she was proud to be next to Nick as they visited their friends and relatives at the tables. Briana had few relatives, and she enjoyed seeing the camaraderie of Nick's brother and two sisters and their spouses. They seemed like such a cheerful and spontaneous group, she was glad to be entering the family. To her surprise, she enjoyed the evening a lot more than she had anticipated, and when the DJ announced the last dance, she was sad to see it end. As they got into Nick's car and were driving away, she waved to those who stayed to see them off.

Nick had planned that they weren't going far. As they entered the expressway he asked her how she felt.

"I'm fine," she answered. "I should be tired but I'm not."

"Me too. I guess I'm too excited," he said, taking one hand off the wheel to caress her arm.

When they reached the hotel, the desk clerk was so friendly that Briana thought that he must know they were just married. They got the key to their room, and Nick carried up the two suitcases. She was nervous, though she didn't want Nick to know it. She found out later that he was nervous too. Nevertheless, they got over their tenseness and spent half the night talking, kissing, and loving.

In the morning, when they walked hand in

hand down the stairs for breakfast, Briana was beaming. She didn't care now who knew that she was married. She glanced at Nick, who just happened to be looking at her and they laughed. He whispered something sweet in her ear. She nodded, and turned to face the late breakfast crowd for the first time as a married woman. It was a very nice feeling.

Strange Tale of Forgotten Love

I don't know how it happened, but last night I was caught in a time warp. Suddenly, I fell into another time and place. When I woke up I was lying in a strange bed. A young woman in unfamiliar dress sat on the edge of the bed. She spoke to me and asked if she could do anything for me. Her language was English, though with an accent that was hard to identify. I told her I didn't know where I was. She stood up, went to the window and drew back the drapes. She invited me to look. I got up and looked out.

"See," she said, "this is Shiitake."

We were several stories up, and I took in the panorama of the large city. Huge, strangely shaped buildings dominated the landscape. Nothing looked familiar. I turned back toward the girl. "I don't know this place."

"It grows on you in time," she said. "There's a lot to do here at night."

"Why are you here?" I asked. "What is your name?"

"I am here to help you," she answered. "My name is Ciapella, Pella for short."

"Pella, you seem like a someone I can talk to. Unfortunately, I am here because of a time warp. I'm afraid I've lost my bearings."

"Maybe I can help you find them."

"I doubt it, but anything's possible."

"Do you know where you were when you lost them?"

"Lost what?"

"Your bearings."

"Oh, that. It's just an expression. It means I don't know where I'm at."

"I told you. You are in Shiitake."

"Shiitake. Never heard of it."

Love Strokes

"You're kidding. You've never heard of Shiitake?"

"No, I'm sorry. I haven't."

"That's OK. Ah, what is your name?"

"I'm Brandon. You can call me Brand for short."

"It's nice to meet you, Brand. Will you be staying long?"

"I don't know, Pella. What year is it here?"

"It's 2794, April the fourth."

"Wow! This is *really* in the future."

"To me it just seems like now. What time are you from?"

"April fifth, 2008.

"Really. Are you a barbarian then?"

"No. I think I'm quite civilized."

"Do you eat animals?"

"Not unless they're cooked."

"Oh, that's disgusting," she replied, making a face.

"You don't?"

"I wouldn't think of it."

"Surprising how things change. Pella, do you think you can help me get back?"

"Back where?"

"To 2008."

"I might be able to," she answered, brushing back a wisp of hair from her face.

"Really? Great! What do we have to do?"

"It's not all that easy, Brand."

"I don't care. I need to get back."

"It's very difficult, Brandon. Besides, I think you'd like it here once you get used to it."

"I doubt it. Please, just tell me what I need to do to get back."

"You have to see Winona."

"Winona?"

"Yes. I don't especially like her, but she's who you have to see."

"She's not evil is she?"

"No, but expensive."

"I have no currency."

"She doesn't use it."

"Then how is she expensive?"

"She takes cells. Specifically, memory cells."

"What on Earth for?"

"She's strange. That's all I can say."

"Does it hurt?"

"No, but you don't remember."

"Oh, I see. Any particular kind of memories?"

"Yes, love memories. She's a romantic at heart," she added softly.

"I see. Is there no other way?"

"Not that I'm aware of, though my friend, Conner, may know another one. It's kind of illegal, you know."

"Hmm." I hesitate, still thinking about losing beautiful memories. "A person can still love, can't they?"

"Yes, new love memories can be formed."

"OK. I guess I'll go with Winona."

"Alright, Brand. Sorry you don't want to stay."

"It's nothing personal. You've been great, Pella"

"Thanks, I guess."

We go to Winona's and say goodbye. I watch her walk away thinking that if she's typical of 2794 then the future isn't going to be too bad.

After all the formalities, some tests, and the cell extraction, I was transported home. Everything looks just as it did before, with one exception. There's a strange woman here, and I have no idea what she is doing in my house. This is what's really peculiar. She says she is my wife. She seems terribly worried, I don't know why.

Epilogue

I should tell you that I've never been against love, just have no recollection of ever thinking about it. The woman *is* rather pretty. . .

"Hi," I begin, in a congenial manner. "So you know me, all about me?"

"Yes, darling," she says, coming over to embrace me. "I love you, Brand," she sighs. "We're going to get through this somehow, honey."

The Mistake

Already, it was getting dark. Opening the door she felt a cool breeze. She put her jacket on and set out. As she walked, the sky turned indigo, and the stars began to appear. First only the bright ones, and then gradually the night sky became filled with twinkling stars. So beautiful. She zipped her coat against the cold, and on the horizon of the distant hill the last vestiges of daylight gave way. Soon it would be totally dark.

The wind began picking up, blowing the trees, and making her feel chill. Already, it was time to return. She made her way back, hunched a little against the strong gusts, her hands in her pockets. Strange, that it was suddenly so windy and not a cloud in the sky. It would take awhile to return, and she looked forward to reaching her warm house.

A person appeared in the distance, a vague shape, nothing more. Whoever it was seemed to tarry, as if waiting for her. Not normally apprehensive, she wondered who it could be. A friend perhaps? Her mind ran through the possibilities. As she came closer, she began to think that it was no one she knew, a stranger.

"Hi, Melissa, remember me?" he said.

She knew the voice immediately. "Tommy," she said as calmly as she could.

"Right, but I prefer Tom now."

"It's been a long time. A very long time."

"Yes, it has. A lot has happened, to me anyway."

"I heard some things, not a lot. Are you out for a walk?"

"You could say that. Mind if I go with you to your house?"

"OK. Where's your car?" she asked.

"It's at the house. Oh, you probably didn't know. I've moved. I'm just up the road at the two-story with the acreage that was for sale."

"You bought that one? I wondered who was going to. A nice piece of land, though the house needs work."

"Yes, outside. The inside's not bad. So, anyway, we're neighbors."

"Imagine that," she said, though her mind was thinking something else. "Here we are already."

"Guess I'll be going."

Melissa hesitated, and then said, "You could come in for a while if you like."

Tom stayed longer than she expected, but she didn't mind. It was nice talking to him. Nothing was said about what had happened before, a long time ago. That was good. She couldn't forget it, but it was better not to talk about it. In fact, she wished she could drive it from her mind.

Melissa had inherited the house and four acres when her parents both died in the tragic auto accident. She liked the rural life, and fortunately she didn't have to drive far to work. Things seemed cleaner in the country, though she was glad she was only miles from town. She went there often, not only to work, but also for some social life. There wasn't much of that nearby.

A week later she saw Tom again. She happened to be walking on the road where he lived, and he must have noticed her because he came out, still putting on a jacket.

"Mind if I join you?" he asked.

"OK."

"Nice night."

"Yeah, not as cold."

"I've been looking at fireplaces. Think I'll install one."

"Really. Do you know how to do that?"

"I think so. I've been studying how to do it. Shouldn't be too hard. It would really warm up the living room on the cold winter days."

"I'd like to see it when you're done."

"By the way, do they celebrate Halloween here?"

"Of course. Children come to trick or treat just as in town. Not as many though. Better get some candy."

"I don't know if I'll be around. There's a costume dance at Homestead. I'm thinking of going, but I have no idea what to wear."

"At Homestead. Yes, I had forgotten about it."

"If you'd be interested we could go together. We'd probably meet some people we know."

"I think Angie and Paula still go. Do you mind if I call one of them and then let you know?"

"That's fine. I'll probably go anyway, so call if you're going and I'll pick you up."

Melissa waited until the next evening to call her friend, Maryanne.

"Hi, Maryanne."

"Lissa, how are you?"

"Fine."

They talked for awhile, and then Melissa brought up Tommy.

"Really. You're seeing him?"

"Kind of. He moved to a house less than half a mile from me and I've run in to him twice walking."

"Has he said anything about. . ." Maryanne hesitated, "you know what I mean."

"No, neither one of us has. Frankly, it's still hard for me to talk about."

"I'm not surprised. So, what do you do when you see him?"

"Well, we've talked some. I even let him in the house."

"Is that a good idea?" Maryanne asked.

"Maybe not. He seems changed, though.

Maybe that time away in the army."

In the end, Maryanne advised caution. Melissa didn't tell her that she was going to the costume dance with him.

It was Halloween night. She had finally decided that she was going to go as a cheerleader. Believe it or not, she still had the pom-poms and the outfit, and she could still fit into it, barely. She also bought a white mask and was just now putting her hair into short, fluffy ponytails when the phone rang. It was Tom.

"I'm ready, are you?"

"Almost. Give me a few more minutes and then come by."

"OK. See you soon."

He arrived about twenty minutes later. "Wow! Do you look striking," she said on seeing him dressed in his rakish pirate costume.

"You sure bring back memories wearing your cheerleading outfit," he said, removing the black patch from his left eye. "You haven't changed a bit."

"Thank you," she said smiling.

She had a wonderful time at the dance. She met several of her old high school friends, and during a break in the music, they did some cheers while others looked on. From time to time she looked out to see Tom, who was standing up next to their table to better see them. She saw him clapping when they finished a cheer. Later, she confided to him that she didn't know what got into her to do it and that she suspected that it was a little too much to drink. He just laughed and said, "You're a natural."

On the way home they talked about the friends they saw, and then they were quiet. She slid over on the pickup seat to be closer to him. When they returned to her house she invited him in. They sat apart from each other, and she offered him cookies and a drink. He had a soda, and they talked for awhile until she felt a little uncomfortable with all the small talk. Finally, she did what she had been wanting to do. She got up and sat down close to him on the sofa. He turned, and in a moment they were in each others arms, kissing. It had been a long time.

She loved it, and she was beginning to think that she loved him. Yet there was something different about it this time. Tom was not caressing her as he had a long time ago. It seemed as if he were holding back.

After a while she asked him, "Is anything wrong?"

He withdrew his arms from her without a word. She asked him again, "Tom, is something the matter?"

He exhaled. "Melissa, I don't want to hurt you. You know what happened before. All you wanted was kissing, and I wanted much more. I wanted to go all the way with you. Even when you resisted, I tried to force myself on you. That was the end of us. I'm sorry it happened that way. I've always been sorry our relationship ended. I promised myself, if I ever got another chance, I'd wait until you were ready. I have to tell you though, it's not easy."

Melissa looked into his eyes, and a tear slid down her cheek. She didn't know what to say. Finally, words came to her. "Tom, I'm sorry too," she said as she put her head against his chest and wrapped her arms tightly around him.

Late that night she couldn't sleep. She was thinking about the evening and seeing everything in a new light. She couldn't wait to see Tom again. She knew now that the lock on her heart had been opened.

From the Oasis

It was a sweltering hot day at the oasis. Along the trails nomads came from every direction to seek its life-giving shelter. The children of the nomads who had already arrived laughed and played in the water. When darkness came, Mariam too, stepped into the water. As she was returning to her father's tent a male voice spoke to her. She turned to see the lithe figure of Budayl blocking her way.

"Budayl," she said, "What are you doing here?"

"I came to see you," he answered.

"If my father knew, he would be angry," she said, eyes flashing.

"I know that but he is an old man and we are young, Mariam."

"What do you want with me, Budayl?" she said, stepping back from him.

"You are a woman; I am a man. I have loved you from the first time I saw you. Come away with me, away from this desert, to a land where the grass is always green."

"Budayl," she said angrily, "you have never spoken to me of love. It is too sudden. I cannot go away with you."

"If that is how it is, I will win your heart a little at a time. I will find sweet smelling night flowers and lay them next to your tent. I will find sparkling stones and leave them by your campfire. I will find the freshest fruits of the desert to lay at your side."

"Oh, Budayl, she answered, moved by his earnestness. "Why did you wait so long to tell me?" She stepped closer to him.

In the darkness Budayl could see her eyes glowing by starlight. He felt her warm breath, and he instinctively put his arms around her and kissed her soft lips. Mariam returned his embrace and kiss with a strength he didn't anticipate, and when the two walked slowly back to her tent, he said, "When you are ready we can go. I have made preparations for the long journey."

"But my father," she hesitated, "I may never see him again."

"Yes, it may be a long time, but when we are settled we can send for him. Then he

Love Strokes

can pitch his tent beside ours and watch his grandchildren play in front of him."

"Oh, Budayl, my heart is so full. I want to come and live with you."

"You make me so happy, my lovely one. Tomorrow let us say goodbye to your father and travel to the land where the grass is always green."

"Yes, I will go with you, Budayl. Tomorrow."

They kissed in front of her tent, and Budayl went back to make final preparations for the journey. When she stepped inside, her father looked up at her and asked, "Have you been seeing Budayl, Mariam?"

"Yes, father, I met him near the water."

"I've seen him looking at you, and I don't like it. Budayl is a different kind of youth."

"He wants to leave the desert, father, to go where the grass is always green."

"He's a dreamer, Mariam. Pay no attention to him."

"I like him, father."

"Sit down, Mariam. Let us talk."

Mariam and her father talked a lot that night. For the first time, her father saw a spirit in her that he had never seen before. Despite all his advice and all his misgivings, he began to understand that she wanted Budayl, and was ready to leave everything to follow him. Ishmael thought to himself, *I should beat her*, but he was weak when it came to his only daughter. In the end, Ishmael gave in.

When Mariam saw that her father was going to let her go, she became very happy. Kissing and hugging her father, she tried to give him some of the love he would be missing when she was gone. Ishmael knew that he might never see his daughter again, and he tried to hold this time with her in his mind, so that he would have happy thoughts when she was gone. He watched her as she went about the tent gathering what she would need for the long journey, and he felt very old. His mind carried him back to the past, when he first met his wife, Areebah. He thought about her and then he went to sleep.

In his sleep he dreamed of Areebah and vividly saw how young and beautiful she was. He saw them together, laughing, dancing, loving. His mind moved to the birth of his daughter and how he held her up and how she looked into his eyes. Then something happened in his dream. There was a crash, lightening, and then darkness and everything was gone.

Slowly, he opened his eyes to see Mariam.

Love Strokes

Already, in the semidarkness of dawn she was up, making her final preparations. She noticed that he was awake, leaning on his elbow. She went to his side and embraced him. "Oh, father, I am sad to say goodbye to you today. You have been so good to me."

Ishmael drew his daughter close and kissed her tenderly on the cheek. "My daughter, my little Mariam. You have been my and your mother's joy for many years and I am sad that you must go. I wish a better life for you on the green grass you speak of and children, beautiful children. I wish you happiness with Budayl."

"Thank you father," she said, clutching him tightly. "Wait. We will send for you. Come and join us when you receive word. I want you to see your grandchildren. I want to see you again."

He held on to both her hands, saying, "Mariam, I am an old man. You have a full life to live ahead of you. Tell me when you have reached the place you speak of. If I am able, I will come."

Budayl led Mariam away from her father's tent. They traveled for several minutes, and in the distance, they could still see Ishmael standing outside his dwelling. They waved a final goodbye and saw him wave back before he disappeared as they rounded a sandy hill.

Their journey was to be long and beset with difficulties, but hope for a better life buoyed them up. The journey across the ocean was terrible, particularly for Mariam, who could not adjust to the movement of the high seas. When at last they landed in New York, more problems beset them. They had relatives there, who loved the big city life, but Budayl and Mariam soon realized that it was not for them. They heard that there were nomads in southern Indiana; so with little more than the clothes on their backs they hitchhiked there. It was the wrong time of year. The biting cold that they were so unused to left them numb and sick, and for days they drifted until at last they found the warming shelter.

"Aunt Betty," as she was called, ran the tiny warming shelter at Green Bottoms, the little Indiana town nestled on the north side of the Ohio River. She operated her establishment from the bankroll of her late husband's river shipping business, and her standards were high. The big sign over the door said it all: "No drinkers, no smokers, no troublemakers, and a shower everyday." She believed that idle hands were the devil's workshop, and she tried to line up jobs that could be done by unskilled workers with local business people. When she saw Budayl and Mariam, she welcomed them.

"My, my, my, look what we've got here. A couple, and by the looks of your tummy, miss, soon to become a family. Welcome to Green Bottoms."

Mariam and Budayl still didn't understand English too well, especially southern twanged English, but they sensed that Aunt Betty was kindhearted, if businesslike.

"Thank you," replied Mariam, with her heavy accent. "Can we little stay, please?"

"For a time yes, honey, if you obey the rules. This is a temporary home, but we help you get started, if you're willing to work."

"Work, yes. We want work. You have job?" asked Mariam.

"Now, that's the kind of answer I like to hear. I can get you work, honey, not the best, but something to put food on the table. Budayl, do you want to work too?" she asked, looking at him closely.

"Yes, yes," he answered. I want work too."

"Good. You have supper, then get cleaned up, try on some fresh clothes, and tomorrow we're going to talk to some people. Antonio here will show you around."

"Thank you much," Mariam said to her before Antonio led them away.

The place was nice, Mariam thought later, as she and Budayl got ready for bed. They even had a small, clean room to themselves. She smiled at Budayl, a rare unworried smile, because she felt that at last things just might work out.

The next day, after breakfast and morning clean up, Aunt Betty called them into her office. She talked to them about what they had done, sized up their English comprehension, and thought about employment options for them. "Do you like cars, Budayl?" She smiled when she saw his reaction.

"Yes, yes. I want car," spoke Budayl with enthusiasm.

"OK. Good. I may be able to get you a job at a lube place. You work under the cars, in a pit changing their oil, etc. Do you know what I'm saying?"

"I don't know," Budayl admitted, losing much of his enthusiasm.

"Well, we'll see when we go there today. Mariam you could wash dishes, clean offices and houses, or maybe care for a young child."

"I like childs," Mariam answered. "And babies," she added with a gleam in her eye.

"I know how care babies."

"You've done it before? Taking care of babies?"

"Yes. In home country."

"I see," Aunt Betty said, thinking out loud. "There are always families needing full time babysitters. If you could get by the language barrier. And if so, it would be a great place to learn English better. Let's look into that."

Mariam didn't understand half of what Aunt Betty said, but she smiled anyway, because she loved babies.

They got dressed up in uncomfortable and unfamiliar warm winter clothes, and Aunt Betty took them outside and told them to get in her car. Budayl sat in front, as he felt it right for a man, and Mariam sat in the back. Budayl patted the dash and told Aunt Betty, "I like cars."

"That's where we're going, Budayl. To a place that services autos."

Soon they were at "Johnson's Lube." Mariam and Budayl stood back while she talked with the owner. They couldn't tell what they were saying, but they saw the man looking toward them. Then the owner and Aunt Betty came over to them.

"So, you are Budayl and you like cars. Is that right?"

"Yes, sir. I much like cars."

"Come with me," he said, motioning to Budayl. He took him to a pit where a car was being serviced by a technician. Then they walked down so that they were underneath the vehicle. "See," he pointed out. "This is changing the oil."

Budayl watched as the technician used a hose to drain the oil from the car, spun off the oil filter, and put on a new one. Then he added fresh oil.

"That's mainly what we do here, Budayl. Over and over again. We also do brakes, air conditioning in the spring and summer, and other things. What do you think?" he asked, looking closely at Budayl.

Budayl didn't understand half of what he said, but he wanted the job so he answered, "I can do."

"Ok, Budayl."

They left the bay area. Budayl returned to stand by Mariam, while Mr. Johnson talked some more with Aunt Betty. She showed him Budayl's card, they nodded, and she returned to where they were standing. "Let's go kids," she said, and they left to go back to her car.

"Hey, you got the job, Budayl. She leaned back and raised her right hand from the wheel to give him a high five. "He's going to try you out." She said a lot of other things that they didn't understand. Then, she drove them away, and they stopped at a big nice-looking house. Aunt Betty rechecked the address, and they got out of the car and walked up the steps to the porch.

Mariam was in awe, as they waited outside after ringing the doorbell. She had never before stood in front of a house so stately. A young woman answered, let them in, and Aunt Betty made introductions. The woman, whose name was Dawn, showed them a large closet where they hung their coats, then led them up a densely carpeted stair. They entered a bedroom decorated in pink with a crib where a small child lay sleeping. Standing next to the crib and looking straight at Mariam, Dawn whispered, "This is Maya."

Mariam came closer, looked down at the peacefully sleeping child, then looked at Dawn and meeting her eyes, she smiled. Dawn spoke to Mariam, asking her some questions to see how much English she understood, and was satisfied. She could tell that Mariam liked babies, particularly her baby.

The rest was all business which Aunt Betty handled competently and quickly. As for Mariam, she was drawn both to Maya and Dawn; and when she realized she was actually going to be given the job, she spontaneously hugged Dawn, in her gratefulness. Immediately afterward, afraid she had been too forward, she looked apprehensively at Dawn, and was relieved to see that she was smiling.

Time passed. At work, Budayl was now called "Bud." He was still at Johnson's Lube and was learning to be a mechanic. He and Mariam had a baby boy, Adan, who was already walking and starting to talk. Finally, things were going well for them in America. Both had jobs and were learning English. They had even put money down to rent a house not far from the river.

Mariam was getting to like this small place in America, and she had made a few friends. Still, she missed her father. She had gotten only one communication from him, sent via Western Union, as he couldn't read or write. There had been no answer to her last two attempts to reach him. She hoped that he got her messages. She hoped that he was OK.

It was springtime in Indiana, the time she loved the most. It was the time of year when she remembered Budayl's words—"A place where the grass is always green." She took her son and the two children she cared for outside and walked the short distance to the river. There, on a hill above the riverbank she sat down and looked out over the magnificent river, breathing in the fragrance of the May flowers and the fresh smell of the earth.

A man, whom she had noticed out of the corner of her eye approached, and she sensed his footsteps in the soft grass. She turned as he came nearer, and her heart leapt when she saw who it was. Jumping to her feet, she ran to him with open arms. They hugged, and she showered him with kisses, then brought him to where the three children played in the grass. They sat down together, and he reached out to pull her child into his arms. Mariam was ecstatic. It was her father.

The Stranger Next Door

She liked it. She had always liked it. It was only when she went to high school that she found out that others thought she was different because of where she lived. Fortunately, she had enough good sense not to be put down by it.

"Little Acres," as it is called, is really part of the city. It is where Kelli had grown up, and it's an area of large lots and small houses. Oh, there are a few big houses also, Reverend Burba's house, for example, but they are the exception. The spacious lots give the area a rural feel; and it is common to see horses, as well as chickens, and even an occasional cow.

Things were changing in Little Acres, however, and Kelli, for one, didn't like to hear about it. But hear it she did, especially from her father. "Why do they want our land?" she would hear him say cantankerously, scratching his head as if he were trying to figure it out. "It's not valuable. Why don't they leave us alone."

"Don't sell, Pa!" she would tell him time and again. "They can't make you sell, can they?"

"Kelli, you don't understand. If they start buying, we have to hurry up and sell. Otherwise we're stuck."

"I don't want to leave! I like it here with my friends!"

At that, her father got up from his chair in front of the TV and walked over to the door and looked out. She knew it meant the conversation was over and she had better not continue. The whole thing remained a mystery to her. Why did they have to move if they didn't want to?

The next day she talked about it with her school friends, Laura and Jill. Laura thought it was cultural. "They don't think and act like us," she explained. "If they come, you sell to stay near your own kind."

"But if people don't sell, why would it make any difference?"

"Yes, I don't understand that either," said Jill.

"Maybe it's a long term type of thing," Laura suggested.

Time passed, Kelli became an upperclassman, and otherwise things didn't change much. Then it happened. The Turner house next door went up for sale after Mr. Turner had a heart attack. It was bought by the people they had heard about, the descendants of the nomads.

It was hardest on her Pa. He would quietly curse, and ball his hands into fists and stare for a long time at the wall. Her mom would come around the back of his chair and massage his neck, trying to make him feel better. It came at a bad time for him because he was on layoff with no certainty that he would be recalled. Consequently, he couldn't put the house up for sale because he couldn't get a loan on another one.

Kelli didn't understand exactly what was going through his mind, but she could sympathize with him. He was her Pa, and she loved him and wished she could cheer him up. At the same time she was interested in the nomad family, especially because there was an older son who looked to be about her age. She was curious about him. Would he act different? She wondered if the whole family would be strange.

Love Strokes

One day, about two weeks after they moved in, Kelli saw the boy next door staring at her. He stared so long, she looked down at herself to make sure she was dressed all right. Then she looked away for a moment before turning back to look at him. He was still staring. She turned away, wondering if he was being rude or if he didn't know any better. Finally, she went inside.

When she thought about it later, she realized that she felt uneasy about him, and yet she didn't want to feel fear on her own porch. She really needed to find out if he was friend or foe. On the next evening, she sat on the porch glider, intent on finding out. She had a book from school that she needed to study two chapters from for a test, and she had her highlighter.

It was a quiet, calm evening; and the sun was in front, low in the sky, giving her plenty of light for reading. She had just about finished and was going to go inside when the door swung open next door. It was him.

She settled herself back on the glider, and pretending to study, she furtively looked over her book at the boy next door. There he was, staring at her again. She didn't want to say "Hi!"—that would have been much too friendly. Instead, she hurled her plastic glass, still half filled with ice, out onto the front lawn. She wondered what he would do. She saw his eyes follow the glass and then they returned to her. However, this time there was a difference. He was smiling.

Kelli had to admit, he looked a lot better smiling than just staring. Nevertheless, she didn't want to get anything started with him, especially with the way her parents were talking, so she got up and went inside. Still, her curiosity made her want to find out more. Several days passed and the evenings began getting cooler.

Then, one day late in September, it was warm again; and as she had nothing special to do that night, she sat out on the porch. She didn't expect to see him. However, he came out right away, as if he had been waiting for her.

He looked at her, and then, as if he had just learned how, he waved. It looked so funny, she laughed. Then, smiling, she waved back. The kid got the biggest grin on his face and started making some motions with his hands. She had no idea what that was about, and she was beginning to wonder if he was retarded or if he didn't know English. She was in a mood to investigate. Ducking her head in the door she yelled to her mother, "Mom, I'm going for a walk. Be back soon." She hoped her mom wouldn't come

Love Strokes

to the front of the house and look out. Then she started walking past the neighbor's house and motioned for him to come. He did.

It was the first of a number of times that they walked together before winter came on, and, before long, she began to like him. Initially, he seemed reserved, though she soon learned he had a sense of humor and had a perspective on many things that was unique and different from that of her friends. She began to feel that she could confide in him. She told him about some of the people she knew, and about her teachers, and even mentioned some things about her parents, like how particular her dad was about the grass. Then winter came, and she was not allowed to walk outside because it got dark too early. She realized she missed the boy next door.

She saw him only briefly after that, because her father was recalled to his job and in February her parents put the house up for sale. It sold fast. Before they moved, she got to talk to him once. She would have given him a goodbye hug, but her parents were also outside and she thought it best not to. Nevertheless, she felt sad, knowing that she might not see him again.

The next year, on her first day at college, she recognized several nomads on campus. Instead of fear, she had a good feeling about them, and she remembered the boy next door. She resolved then, that as soon as she could get a ride, she was going back to see him.

BRIDESTAR

The star ship moved silently toward the Earth-sized green planet, fourth from its sun. The small, yellow star had long since been catalogued, but like most, its planets had never been explored.

Nick Bartok opened his eyes carefully; he was not used to the bright sunlight. Suddenly, he jumped out of bed and rushed to the terrestrial energy monitor. Had he seen a momentary blip? He stood there, watching, feeling foolish as he stared at the empty screen. No civilization had evolved on this planet; they knew that, didn't they?

He and his partner, Matthew Kerry, had traveled two months through space to reach this destination, and now their long journey would pay off. He knew that he was being optimistic. In reality, the chance of finding usable crude was always less than fifty percent, and less than that of finding enough oil to be profitable to extract. Still, he, Matt, and the team had studied the charts carefully, had minutely analyzed the spectrographic data, and had applied all the known mathematical formulae and computer analyses to pick out this particular spot in the galaxy. He was proud of their team, and it had been personally hard for him to say goodbye. He thought of Terri, and he remembered how her eyes filled with tears as they kissed their farewell. He thought again of the last thing she whispered. "Please be careful Nick. Come back to me."

"Oh, that light!" groaned Matt as he wakened, covering his eyes with his hands to shield them from the sun.

Nick pressed the shade activator, saying, "Take a look down there, Matt. Have you ever seen such a lush planet?"

Beneath them, white-capped, majestic clouds framed the emerald green flora of Bridestar. They could sense already the freshness and the untainted atmosphere of a planet untouched by man.

"It's magnificent," agreed Matt, opening the shades further so he could see clearly. "Let's eat breakfast now, so we'll be ready to leave the ship when we land."

Nick still marveled at the technology that made meal selections so varied. Growing up, his breakfast choice was usually cereal or toast, and often only toast. Milk was frequently not available. "What would you like?" he asked Matt, as he eyed the breakfast menu that appeared on the smooth wall of the restant.

"Croissants, quiche, and tropical fruit," Matt answered.

"What?" said Nick, turning around.

"I'm joking," Matt said, with a grin. "Ham and eggs sounds good to me." He turned back to the orbital tracking readouts.

By the time they finished eating, they had the information needed for landing. The onboard computers provided topographic maps and coordinates specifying initial target areas for oil exploration. Continuing the quiet descent toward the planet, they noted that clouds began to obscure the sun. They dropped the last few hundred yards and felt the unmistakable jolt of landing.

Dawn was just breaking on the planet, and

as the light increased, they saw that they had landed in an area with long grasses and scattered trees. Nick opened the hatch and they looked out. The aroma of verdant grassland pervaded the cabin. It was incomparably better than the continuously recycled air they had been breathing for so long.

"Mm! Smell that air," said Matt, inhaling deeply. Stepping to the ground, he moved his arms up and down, turned, and jumped twice to test the gravity. Nick followed; walking out a short distance, he checked the landscape both near and far with a practiced eye.

Despite his training to approach a new environment with caution, he began to feel a sense of giddiness, which he attributed to the high oxygen content of the air. Instead of setting up their instruments, he wanted to explore first-hand their surroundings. The more he thought about it, the more the idea grew on him. "What the hell," he mumbled to himself, thinking about how long they had been cooped up before their arrival.

"Matt, let's take a walk."

"Immediately, before we set up the equipment?"

"That's what I'm thinking. We can pack a lunch, stretch our legs, and see what's out there."

"Fine with me. We can do the setup when we return."

Soon they were on their way, each with a sidearm attached to his belt. They walked away from the ship, through the grass and trees, in the general direction of some low hills in the distance.

They continued quietly for a time, taking note of their surroundings. Nick was the first to speak. "Matt, to me there's something unusual about this place. Not only is it beautiful, but it also seems extremely familiar. It's as if we had landed inadvertently on an unknown and undeveloped place on Earth."

"I know what you mean. There *is* something about it. It's as if we've been here before."

They walked further, taking a closer look at plant specimens that resembled those they knew from home. They were startled when they fleetingly glimpsed what appeared to be a deer, though it moved too fast for them to positively identify it. Finally, Matt said, "I'm not used to this much hiking. Let's stop and have lunch."

Nick pointed to a spot where the grass was shorter. They moved there and sat down. Soon, they were enjoying their lunch, and basking in the warm afternoon sun.

"I feel like taking a nap," Matt said, stretching his legs.

"Go ahead." Nick settled himself against a fallen tree trunk. "I'll keep watch, although I don't think we have anything to worry about." He looked toward the nearby pond and wondered lazily what kind of aquatic life it might contain. Soon, he was asleep.

A young woman appeared near some trees at the edge of the pond. She soundlessly disrobed and purposefully walked into the water. She was lovely, of average size, with full curves and a slender waist. Her long dark hair fell down her back, and she stood for a moment in shallow water. Then she turned in Nick's direction, tilted her head as if she saw him, and turned back. She didn't seem at all surprised, if she did indeed see him. She moved again and, with a brief backward glance, walked out into deeper water.

"Nick. Wake up." Nick felt Matt shaking his shoulder. "We've got to get back to the ship before nightfall."

"What? OK." Gradually Nick remembered where he was. "What a dream I had! I saw a gorgeous girl bathing in that pond over there. She undressed first and started walking into the water. Then, she turned and seemed to look right at me. It was as if she was inviting me to join her."

"Nick, we've both been away from women too long."

"It's just that she seemed so real. I'm going over there to see if there's any trace of her."

They walked the short distance to the lake. Near it, they saw something unusual.

"Look at that," exclaimed Matt. "It looks like a road."

Nick pressed his heel into the dark green surface. "Like a road, and yet spongy and yielding."

Kneeling down, Matt rubbed the surface with his fingers. "It appears to be made of some kind of dense vegetative matter."

Nick turned to look along each direction of the roadway. "I wonder where it leads?" he speculated.

"We've definitely found something else here besides oil," Matt asserted, automatically placing his hand on the holster of his pulsar. "I wonder if they know we're here?"

"They might, but I doubt it. Otherwise, they could easily have come to meet us. Or, for that matter, they could have attacked. They must be at a very low level of civilization," Nick continued, "or our energy monitors would have detected spent gases in their atmosphere."

"This road doesn't look very primitive to me."

"No, it doesn't. I'd love to have a mass analyzer here to feed a chunk of this into."

"We'd better get back to the ship right away," said Matt, obviously alarmed.

"Yes. Let's split up and travel about fifty meters apart. That way it would be hard for them to ambush us both, and we can help each other if necessary.

"OK," Matt replied, removing his pulsar from its holster. They cautiously made their way toward the star ship, keeping each other in sight and watching for anything that moved. They had a momentary scare when another of the deer-like creatures jumped out from some bushes, but otherwise they saw nothing unusual.

Back inside the ship, with the perimeter alarm system turned on, they felt less tense. Nightfall settled over the land, and after a satisfying supper, they were ready to make plans for the next day. Realizing that they had not exercised sufficient caution, they were glad there had been no negative consequences. With complex life forms known to be on the planet, they would have to be careful.

Nick wondered if the girl in his dream was real or had been imagined. Either way, it wouldn't change what they needed to do. They had to find out if there were any aliens living nearby that might be a security concern. The ship's firepower, they knew, would be able to withstand anything except the most powerful attack. Nevertheless, they couldn't proceed with oil exploration if the natives were hostile.

Nick and Matt were prepared to kill any animals that got in their way, but killing aliens was something else. Not only was it not authorized, but to Nick it was not even to be contemplated. Explorers were allowed to bargain with natives within certain limits. However, negotiations often proved difficult, as scientists usually had no special skill in dealing with unknown cultures and had no authorization to offer gifts or royalties. Nick and Matt discussed these considerations until late that evening. When they were ready to turn in, they knew clearly what they needed to do the next day.

After falling asleep, Nick again had a dream. He saw the same girl, who this time appeared to be in a house. She seemed to be trying to tell him something. There was an indistinctness about the vision, although he had the impression that it had something to do with the green road. The last thing that he sensed was a message that said, "Come, there is nothing to fear."

They awoke refreshed in the morning, and the sunshine and wide, undisturbed vista made them feel less apprehensive. After breakfast, their plan was to take their vehicle, the amcar, and drive back to the green road. Once there, they wanted to cut a piece of its surface for analysis, and then follow it to wherever it led.
Traveling by car was much safer, as its sensors could be set to detect life forms, and they could speed away if anything threatened. After taking the normal precaution of setting the ship's internal and perimeter protective system, they stepped into their vehicle, and soon were zipping over the grasslands heading back toward the pond.

"I like this little convertible," said Nick. "It may be old, but it maneuvers well, and you still retain a lot of control."

"Yes," agreed Matt. "The newer models are so smooth and automated they make you feel like a passenger in your own car."

"Look, there's the lake," said Nick. "And over there is the road." He switched off the accelerator. They coasted down, landing near the water. They cautiously surveyed the area before getting out of the vehicle. Nick knelt down to examine the road while Matt kept watch. He found the dark green surface hard to extract, but using the sharp side of a rock hammer, he managed to remove a piece from the edge.

"Look at this, Matt. The top is green, but the middle section is creamy white, and the bottom is dark brown. I'm not sure if the surface is something that's sprayed on or if it's a natural part of the substance." He handed it to Matt.

He looked it over carefully. "Unusual. It has the same texture throughout, just different levels of color." He handed it back to Nick, who put it in a compartment in the car.

"Well, what do you think?" asked Nick. "Are you ready to visit the natives?"

"Why not?" Matt answered, taking a deep breath. "It will be very interesting to see what they look like."

They put the top up and slowly drove down the road, staying on high alert since they didn't know what might be waiting for them.

They realized that if there were only a few aliens, or if they were friendly, their mission need not be compromised. However, if the inhabitants became scared, and resolved to fight, their stay on the planet would have to be terminated. Hopefully, they could at least do some preliminary testing first to determine if there was enough oil to warrant a return trip. If there was, a diplomatic party would be dispatched to negotiate with the natives. The goal, of course, was to convince them to give up the oil, with gifts and incentives for doing so. Usually that was effective.

If, however, the natives didn't agree, their rights were often ursurped. Not by the Worlds' Organization itself, but by pirates who sometimes found undeveloped sites by breaking through encrypted communications. Unfortunately, those thugs cared little for life when the black market oil trade was so lucrative.

They continued down the roadway, and it wasn't long before they saw structures in the distance. As they drew closer, it was clear that the structures were dwellings nestled on the outskirts of a large village. The houses were of unusual architecture with rounded sides and slanting roofs that were all canted in the same direction. They were low lying; in fact, most were at least partially surrounded by earthen embankments. There were open grassy areas between the houses, and a stream flowed along the edge of the town. It was an idyllic scene.

"Look at that," Nick exclaimed. "I don't believe my eyes."

"Neither do I," echoed Matt. "Except for the rounded houses, it looks like a scene from the eighteenth century. I think that may be a mill wheel over there by the stream."

"Of course. They must actually grind their grain there. How picturesque, harnessing water power just like we used to do hundreds of years ago."

"Don't let your guard down too soon, Nick. They may come at us with pitchforks."

"Or worse," Nick agreed. "They may have discovered gunpowder. We need to move the amcar and conceal it well off the road. Then we can investigate further before we attempt communication."

"I hate to leave it behind, but you're right. Chances are it would only scare them. I wonder what form of transportation they use?"

The question was no sooner asked than it was answered. Appearing around a bend in the road, two figures were fast approaching them. They rode large animals that combined a cat-like head on a large, deer-like body. Quickly reaching for their pulsars, they moved to the side. Unfortunately, there was no time to hide. They had already been spotted. They saw that the two riders were women and in a moment the women were standing before them.

Nick was speechless. The dark-haired girl he had seen in his dream surveyed him from her mount. Her eyes seemed to bore through him. Somehow, he felt she knew what he was thinking. His own eyes were riveted on hers, so much so that everything else was a blur. In the background, he heard Matt shouting something. Whatever he said, the words didn't register on his consciousness.

The girl dismounted, and now she was standing directly in front of him. She placed her hand on his arm. Immediately, the thoughts he had of fighting or fleeing dissolved. Looking at her, he realized that she was speaking to him. Without words, she was telling him to follow her. Instantly, all the reasons he might have for resisting her wish vanished from his mind. When she remounted, Nick turned to Matt and said, "Let's follow them into town."

"Are you sure?"

"Yes."

As they returned to the amcar Nick

explained. "They want to meet us and are welcoming us to come with them to their village."

"OK. I just hope we're not taking any unnecessary chances."

"I believe they can be trusted."

"I'm not so sure, Nick. On the other hand, it seems unlikely that two women and a child would be sent out for what could be a dangerous mission."

"A child?" asked Nick. "Did you say they had a child with them?"

"Yes, didn't you see? The woman on my side of the road had a little girl riding with her. Probably not more than three or four years old."

Nick directed the car to follow the riders at a safe distance. Soon, they reached the first houses. They took the precaution of moving their vehicle to a small copse of trees nearby, and then caught up with and followed the women into one of the houses.

The next few hours went by like minutes for Nick. He spent the whole time with the young woman, whose name, he learned, was Tara. Within the walls of her own house, she seemed even more charming. He guessed her age to be about twenty-two. She wore a soft leather dress that was cinched around her waist with a thong. The garment reached to her knees. She had on a pair of thin brown shoes, also made of leather, and wore no jewelry or other ornamentation. She was several inches shorter than him, had an excellent figure and fairly long fingers. She looked as if she could have come from Earth.

Nick didn't understand at first how he seemed to be able to communicate with her. He certainly didn't know the language. Was he somehow reading her thoughts? Her voice was melodic, and she used her hands frequently as she talked.

He concentrated, watching her, and abruptly understood that she was telling him not to focus on the words, but on the meaning. He began to understand what she was saying to him; that communication required emptying his mind of preconceptions, looking directly into her eyes, and letting his consciousness read hers. In time he got better at it, though he began to realize that he was letting himself become mesmerized by the beauty of her eyes.

"Nick. Nick!" Matt's strident voice broke through his concentration.

"We better leave," Matt said with insistence. "It's getting late."

"OK," he answered. Turning to Tara, he

expressed to her that he had to leave and saw that she understood. She followed them to the door, and he held her hand a moment before they went out. He told her that he would return.

They pulled away from Crystal, the name of the town, and Nick was quiet, thinking about Tara. Matt must have had thoughts of his own, because on the short trip back he didn't interrupt his reverie. Once inside the ship, or space module, as it was often called, Nick ordered hot onion soup, bread, and coffee from the synthesizer. He waited until Matt's food was ready and they both sat down to eat. Nick was starting his second cup of coffee when Matt leaned toward him and said, "Nick, we need to talk. I don't understand you. I mean, what is it with the girl? Have you completely forgotten why we're here?"

Nick was surprised. As he looked at Matt he realized he was serious. "What do you mean?"

"Nick you've been acting like a kid ever since we came to this planet. I admit that I went along with it at first. But today, when you let that girl order you around, and then spent hours looking into her eyes like a lovesick teen, it became obvious to me that something is wrong. Are you remembering that we have a job to do here? Have you forgotten about Terri?"

Nick realized that although Nick had been there with him, he had not experienced what he had. Apparently, Matt had not communicated with them at all. Not knowing where to start, he proceeded to try to explain to him what happened from his perspective. "Matt, you may not understand right away what I have to tell you, but hear me out. First, let me ask you, what did *you* see when we were in the house."

"I saw three aliens, two females and a child. They could have passed for human except that they had rather long fingers. The house we entered was simple, with only basic wooden furniture, cushioned with fabric and animal skin. There was a wood-burning stove in the kitchen, and water was brought in from an outside well. The other female, the one with the child, kept trying to look into my eyes. I looked away, not wanting to be mesmerized as you seemed to be."

"The child with them was cute and playful, and tried to get my attention." He paused to take a drink and then continued. "I wanted to keep a look out for what was going on outside to make sure that no crowds were gathering. At first, everything seemed normal. Some natives passed by, and they didn't stop. Then I saw two of the aliens holding onto another one, apparently taking him somewhere. I didn't know what that was about, but I knew it was time for us to leave."

"That's something I didn't see," Nick reflected. "I'm curious about it."

"I was a lot more than curious," Matt replied, irritated by Nick's speculative manner. "We don't know what these humanoids might be up to. Things with them may not be what they appear to be on the surface."

"Matt, you don't understand. I was able to talk with them. You see, they can communicate in a way that we don't. That's why the woman was trying to make eye contact with you. They converse by thought transference, similar to mental telepathy. It wasn't easy, but with Tara's help, I was able to do it too. The process requires eye to eye contact. I wasn't just staring into her eyes; I was actually talking to her."

"Really? And what exactly were you talking about?" asked Matt with irony in his voice.

"Different things. She told me that her name is Tara, and that she teaches, and also works at a medical facility. She told me about their culture. I learned, for example, why our sensors couldn't pick up any signs of energy. They are solar powered. That's why all the house roofs slant in one direction, toward the sun. They have rock storage systems built under their floors that radiate heat when the sun doesn't shine. Their climate is moderate, with no extremely cold or hot weather. During warm weather they use sliding shutters to the block the sun's rays."

"As for their economy, it's rustic and unsophisticated. They fish at the stream and at a nearby lake. They raise sheep-like animals for food and use their wool and skins to make clothing. They also plant vegetable crops and harvest cereal grains that they grind and make into bread. They even raise a crop that's similar to cotton. For the most part, they have the same kind of crafts that have been known since at least the days of the Roman Empire. There's a blacksmith, shoemakers, a milliner, instructors, butchers, potters, carpenters, a cooper, and, of course, a brewer."

"Tara explained that the children, and even some adults, can't speak by thought transference. Most, however, begin to acquire the ability by the time they reach their middle to late teens. It's important to remove any preconceptions from one's consciousness so that another's thoughts can be perceived. I think the process came easier for me because I was attracted to Tara from the beginning."

"You certainly were. That was obvious. Unfortunately, it may also be the problem. These aliens have some mental powers that we know little about. Do you realize the danger we are in if they are able to control our conscious thoughts? It's possible that the whole scene in front of us may only be a figment of our imagination, an idyllic world created out of our own cultural memories. Remember how we both noted how similar their world is to ours, including almost identical grass and trees? If they can do that, they can also make our minds think that they look just like humans."

"That's crazy. The way you're talking, I wouldn't be surprised to hear you say that Tara is really a scorpion in disguise! Really Matt, I think you've been reading too much science fantasy. I've read stories like that myself, but we and our predecessors have explored thousands of worlds, and found hundreds with advanced life forms. Nowhere have we found anything other than what we perceived it to be."

"Are you sure about that? What about the third planet of Borigidor?" Scientists still don't know what's there because each team of experts sent to investigate it comes back with different observations."

"Yes, I've heard of the planet. The anomaly appears to be caused somehow by the constant mists and its multiple suns. I definitely believe, and all the historical data supports me, that what we're seeing now is really here, and that what I touch and feel is reality."

"Don't you see," insisted Matt, "that we are here on an important mission to find oil for the eastern half of the galaxy, which desperately needs it. Despite that, you've suddenly lost interest. That's not like you. Our company has a lot of money invested in this mission. They don't expect us to be sidelined by the native girls."

Stung by Matt's remarks, Nick walked out of the cabin and stepped outside. He gazed at the grass and the trees within range of the perimeter lights surrounding the module. Going a little further, he pulled up some blades of grass, and rolled their stems between his thumb and fingers. He came to a tree, leaned against it, and felt its solid mass. Then, he looked back at the ship and thought about the two month voyage that brought them here. Somehow, it seemed like a long time ago.

Right now, he felt like walking, walking through the night, continuing, until he found the road that would take him back to the village, back to Tara. "Wait. What am I thinking?" he asked himself. "Why am I suddenly having these feelings for a woman I've met once?" He began to wonder if he was indeed being manipulated. On further consideration, he realized that he really didn't know. He still thought Matt was wrong about things not being what they seemed. However, he was right about one thing. No matter how he felt about Tara, it was time to get to work. He returned to the ship and entered the cabin. Matt was there, looking over some charts. He said to him, "Better get some sleep, Matt. We've got a lot of work to do tomorrow."

Tom Molnar
120

Chapter Two

The days that followed were filled with exploration and analysis of the data generated by their instrumentation. They took the amcar to several more distant sites to study geological formations of porous and impermeable rock. The place where their ship landed was in a former sedimentary basin, which eons ago had been under a swampy sea. The vegetation that had grown there for millions of years gradually dropped to the bottom as it died. The water level had risen, and in time, all the accumulated vegetation was covered over and compressed by layers of silt, which in time became rock.

Eventually, the tremendous pressure of the silt, rock and water caused the decayed vegetation to turn into oil and gas. The same thing happened on Earth and on other planets with sufficient warmth, vegetation, and oxygen. Man's voracious appetite for this "black gold" to power his machinery and heat his dwellings had created a demand unequal to the supply.

There had been warnings of shortages as far back as the twentieth century, when the Arabians briefly cornered the market. For a time, nuclear power was seen as a viable alternative until there were a series of accidents leading to the disastrous total meltdown in Botswana. It was estimated at the time that the explosion killed over two million people instantly, and that tens of millions more suffered an agonizing and slow death.

The dark winds that blew from the ashes infected the rest of the world, causing cancer rates to escalate around the globe for the next fifty years. Botswana itself was uninhabitable for a hundred years, and parts of Africa, and even Madagascar had to be evacuated for twenty years. Of course, there were foolish inhabitants who refused to be moved. They paid with their lives for their intransigence.

That was a long time ago, and for over two hundred years since then nations and planets had relied on oil, with the expectation that the new worlds brought into the supply nexus would always meet the demand. Unfortunately, that assumption was unproven, and as virgin oil fields seemed harder and harder to find, the cries for conservation and even a return to nuclear energy were again being heard. Scientists were hard at work trying to find substitute forms of energy, but as yet no inexpensive energy source had been developed.

That's why Nick and Matt were here, on this distant planet of another star, many light years from home. Highly paid geologists, they had to give up months of their lives in tedious space travel to make the round trip to this destination. The reward, however, was such that one good oil strike would make them well known and financially independent for the rest of their lives.

Nick had already been in deep space four times and had found nothing. He promised himself that this was his last trip. He had enjoyed seeing other worlds and the cosmopolitan ambiance of the space centers, but he realized now that he was ready to settle down. He thought about Terri, whom he knew would be awaiting his return. Matt interrupted his reverie.

"Nick, what do you want to do tomorrow on our day off?"

"I don't know. I've thought about it, but nothing interesting comes to mind. How about you?"

"Yeah, I don't know either. I'm not sure if I want to see another movie or play a simgame or both. I do plan to relax with my favorite drink."

"I'm getting tired of everything simulated," Nick answered. "Maybe I'll just read a book and take a walk. Are you ready to wrap it up for today?"

"We might as well. There's not much more we can do before it gets dark. Next week I think we'll be ready to take some core samples and analyze them. The preliminary findings in sectors 31 and 38 definitely look promising."

They packed up their equipment, dusted off their clothes, got into the car, and headed back to the ship.

It had long become standard practice in the oil industry, even in the outposts, to take one day a week off. Without a day to rest, tensions could build to the detriment of the work and the team relationships. All modern ships took the need for recreation into account. Most had digital libraries, movies, and play and game simulators, which recreated the originals with satisfying authenticity. With the sport simulator, for example, one could participate in almost any sport, and even experience specific muscle and tendon injuries, like "tennis elbow" if overdone. In the library, memory banks provided the literature of the world,

Love Strokes

and in seconds a selection could be downloaded to a pocket reader.

Although starships, through computerization, carried the world with them, there remained one major deficiency. Other than one's partner, there were no real people with which to interact. Nick missed that companionship more and more. In fact, he was not far from admitting to himself that he was lonely. At twenty-seven, he knew that he wanted someone real, warm, and affectionate to be part of his life.

The morning dawned bright and cool, with the prospect of temperatures rising during the day. Matt slept in. Nick ate breakfast and attended a short, recorded service. He stretched his legs and decided to take a long hike. He enjoyed walking. It helped him to take his mind off the job, and it was good exercise. He began striding toward the morning sun but turned left as another thought entered his mind. In less than an hour he found the green road. He smiled and continued walking. Now, he knew exactly where he was going.

What was it about her that attracted him so much? He tried to analyze it. Was it only the loneliness of too many long trips away from home? No, that wasn't it, he assured himself. There was something about her that affected him like no one else had, not even Terri. He had recognized that when they were together at the house. Now, he had to go back to find out more about her.

Soon the town stretched out in front of him as he stood on a rise in the road. Then, to his surprise, he saw her. She was walking across his line of view, slowly, with her hands clasped together in front of her as if in a reverie. He called her name. She looked toward him, and instantly he felt a warm message of welcome. They moved quickly to each other, and as they met he instinctively put his arms around her, drawing her close. She looked up into his eyes, her long, silky hair framing her face, and asked why he hadn't come sooner. He realized that she had missed him. He laughed softly at the intensity of her feelings and felt a tenderness toward her that was new to him. He proceeded to explain to her the importance of his work and how he had to fight to ignore his thoughts of her during the week. Now that he was in her presence again, he felt happier, with a lightheartedness he hadn't experienced for a long time. He liked the lilting richness of her voice and the way the words seemed to flow musically together. She gestured often with her hands for emphasis, and though Nick didn't understand everything she said, he got the main ideas.

Love Strokes

As they continued walking, she talked about her family and mentioned that her parents had both died. She was anxious for him to meet her grandfather, who lived nearby, and to get to know her sister and her daughter. She wanted to learn more about him, how he had come from another world, and what it was like on Earth. She asked about his family, and wondered what women on Earth were like.

She had so many questions. Nick started by telling her how they had spent two long months in space navigating to the planet by means of their galactic starship. She was amazed to learn that he had come so far, from a distant sun, and had difficulty conceiving of a vehicle that could travel for so long a distance through the dark and cold in the complete absence of air. She was childlike in her total lack of knowledge of space and other worlds.

Nick told her about Earth and its huge cities with skyscrapers over a thousand feet tall, and of its underground highways and towns. He described the teaming multitudes of people in the large cities and the relative sparseness that still remained in some parts of the land. He related to her how the Worlds' Organization had acted to quash major wars between nations and how long ago it had banned all major weapons systems. He acknowledged that conflicts still broke out from time to time, usually over old disputes or unsettled boundaries.

Nick told her it was deplorable that nations still hadn't really learned to live together, but he was glad that at least dissident nations no longer had the power to destroy entire populations. The Worlds' Court schedule was always full, and the one hundred men and women from all the major planets and countries who sat on it made some unpopular decisions, but Nick felt that it was the best alternative to internecine warfare.

Tara seemed much more interested when he talked, at her request, about the women of Earth. She was astonished when he described some of the fashions that were currently in vogue, including the way women coiffured their hair. Nick could see how Tara was trying to visualize herself wearing the styles he was describing, and he knew she would like to see them.

"Someday I'll take you to the ship, and you can see for yourself on EV." He tried to explain briefly how that worked, and ended up saying, "I really like the way you look now, nothing artificial."

"Now, yes. But people get tired of the same thing after awhile."

" I wouldn't."

"I know what," she said. "I could dye my hair ochre and wear it up on my head, like this."

He laughed as she piled her dark hair on top of her head and grinned at him. "Maybe I won't show you those films," he said half seriously. "I don't want to corrupt you."

Abruptly, she made a mock pouting face.

"OK, I'll show you some films, but first I should introduce you to my partner, Matt. He'll want to get acquainted with you before we do anything at the ship."

Just then they were interrupted by a call. A middle-aged woman, coming from the gristmill, recognized Tara and hailed her. She waved, and while still approaching, began speaking animatedly. Then she paused, looked into Nick's eyes, and extended her hand. Nick read her clearly. She said, "pleased to meet you." Nick grasped her hand and mentally said, "My pleasure." She took his hand, and instead of shaking up and down, she drew it back and forth, in a sawing motion. Then she turned to talk some more with Tara. After chatting a short while, she again looked at Nick and said, "Goodbye."

"That was Mrs. Marferti," said Tara. "She's an old friend of my mother. She doesn't have any children of her own and has always been close to Shari and me, especially since mother died."

"What did she die of?" he asked, as they walked toward her house.

"The same thing most people die of."

"What is that?" he asked.

"Her heart. Isn't it the same on Earth?"

"No, not at all. On Earth, people die from many different things. Besides heart attacks, there are strokes, pneumonia, emphysema, various diseases, and even cancer."

"Really. Do they have to suffer then at the end?"

"Yes, they often do, and sometimes for a long while. Fortunately, most can be helped with medication so that it goes a lot easier. How is it for people here?"

"Most of the time it comes suddenly, with heart pain. At other times, it goes on for a few days or even weeks. Both my mother and father died suddenly."

"I'm sorry."

"Thank you. Much has happened since then. At first, I missed them terribly, but I've gotten over it, and it helps to know I'll eventually see them again." She waved to a neighbor as they reached the door of her sister's house. When they entered, Shari greeted them at the door, and her little girl, Neena, ran in from the kitchen to meet them.

"Hi, Neena. How's my big ampasso?" asked Tara, as she lifted the girl into her arms. Neena began chattering excitedly as they walked further into the house.

The room they entered was large, with a high ceiling, and was illuminated mostly by big windows on two sides. A candelabrum, centered in the middle of the table, lit the place settings.

"You're just in time for dinner," said Shari, as she tended some crocks at the stove.

"Did I hear dinner announced?" a deep voice responded from another room.

"Yes, grandpa, you might as well come now," Shari answered. "We have a guest who will be eating with us today."

"You *will* stay for dinner, won't you?" asked Tara, turning to look at Nick.

"I'd be happy to. I haven't eaten real, unprocessed food for a long time."

"Hello, young man," said Tara's grandfather, extending his hand to Nick as he entered the room. He was tall, husky, and white-haired, with a friendly demeanor. As Nick looked at him, thoughts in the nature of, "Glad to meet you," registered in his consciousness. They shook hands and Nick replied similarly, "Glad to meet you, sir."

The mind connection seemed to be working because he answered, "Just call me Ruskin. I've heard you've come from another planet far away from here." He hesitated a moment. "It's so hard to believe that it's really possible," he said, with evident astonishment.

"You can talk to him about it later, grandpa," said Tara. "I think Shari's ready with dinner."

Nick watched as they bowed their heads and then passed the steaming bowls around the table. Tara sat at Nick's right and told him about the different dishes as they came to them. The contents of two of the bowls looked familiar; one of them looked liked potatoes, and the other could have been carrots. All the food was hot, and most of it was delicious although one salad dish had an unusual taste that he didn't savor.

Ruskin tended to monopolize the conversation, keen as he was to learn all about the space trip, life on other worlds, and their project on Bridestar. Nick had some trouble at first understanding what the older man was saying, but Tara helped, and he got better at it after a while. He learned that Ruskin was one of two herbalists in the town, and that he grew and prepared extracts for medicinal purposes. Nick had had a passing interest in biology years before entering the space program, which helped him to understand what he was saying, although Tara frequently needed to interpret. At length she said, "It's getting late already, and it's dangerous to travel after dark at this time of year. Would you stay over with us until morning?"

Nick looked at his chronograph. "No thank you," he answered. "I'd like to, but Matt would be worried if I didn't come back tonight. Why do you think traveling at night is dangerous?"

She explained to him that the mating season of the Great Thorns begins at about this time every year. "It's the time when the male birds set out on extended flights far from their cliff-side rookeries. They travel silently in the night, searching for large prey. When they find it, they swoop down, plunge their long sword-like beak into the unfortunate creature, and carry it back to their lair. Their quest is driven not by hunger, but by their eagerness to prove their prowess to a female. At the height of the mating season they will sometimes hunt even during the day."

"Don't worry about me, Tara," Nick was quick to assert. "No bird would stand a chance against my pulsar."

"If you must go, I'll walk you to the end of town." She thought a moment. "I know. You could take my forc."

Nick thought about the animal that he had seen her riding. "Thank you, but I'd rather walk," he said.

"Then I'll go with you a short distance."

They went quietly along the stream that bordered the village.

"What do you think of my grandfather?"

"He's an interesting person. I was surprised at how much he knows about natural medicine. If he had modern laboratory equipment, who knows what kind of breakthroughs he might make."

"Oh, he does have a laboratory. I'm sure he'd like to show it to you sometime."

They came to the outskirts of town all too fast, and it was time to say goodbye. He kissed her, and she returned the kiss. As they parted, she asked when she would see him again. "Soon," he answered.

He proceeded down the green road away from her, and when he came to a bend, he turned to see her still standing there. He waved, then continued on. Suddenly he fell to the ground. He wasn't hurt, but his head felt like it was turning without his body and he could scarcely move his limbs. It was the last thing he remembered.

Chapter Three

At the starship, Matt paced back and forth. It was after eleven p.m. by synchronized Earth time, and there was still no sign of Nick. Matt's earlier irritation was now changing to fear. He had guessed that Nick might have gone to visit Tara, but it was unlike him not to be back by now.

Midnight. Still no sign of him. He began to fear the worst. He imagined that Nick had been deluded by their mental deception, and now he was hurt or captured. Maybe they had even taken control of his mind. If he wasn't hurt, could he be trusted? Matt turned up the sensitivity of the ships perimeter protection system. One a.m. He thought seriously of alerting the Space Patrol. Though they might never respond this far away from their rounds, at least there would be a record in case he didn't make it back. One thirty. He sent the message to alert the Patrol. Then he realized how foolish that was. Even if they got the report, it would take them over a month to respond. At this distance, they simply wouldn't do anything except record it until an outer boundary ship happened along.

Two a.m. *Wait, he thought to himself. They don't know anything about the firepower I have on this ship. They apparently don't even have guns. With two hand pulsars, I could stand off a hundred of them.* He began to take courage. It was obvious to him that the aliens could win only by mental deception, and now he was alert to it.

Matt knew that his next step was to find out what happened to Nick. He coolly resolved that if they had killed him they would pay dearly for it. If, instead, they had captured him, he felt certain that he could rescue him by force of arms. Even if Nick's consciousness was under their control, Matt thought that if he could bring him back to the ship, he could get him out of their power.

He decided that he would wait until early dawn to attack. In the interim, he tried sleeping, but it was no use. His consciousness was alerted, and almost automatically it projected him into different scenarios so that he could decide how to react, regardless of the situation. Finally, he saw the first faint light of day through the window. He munched on an energy bar while strapping on two pulsars. Then he got into the amcar and pressed the accelerator. He was traveling over the trees at high speed, and soon the town appeared in view. He slowed down to look for the house and quickly found it. Then he parked the car in a nearby thicket.

The day was just dawning, and it was still dusky in the town. No one seemed to be about. As he silently approached the house, he steeled his mind so as not to come under their influence. He held a pulsar in each hand. An animal made a low sound that startled him. It was one of those strange creatures that they use for transport. He reached the door and found it unlocked. He quietly pushed in. Entering, he found that he was in the dining area. He heard nothing. He crossed the room and stopped, listening intently for the slightest sound, snoring, breathing, anything. Then, from an upper room, he heard something indecipherable. It sounded like a shudder, followed immediately by a gasp.

Love Strokes

He hesitated a moment, then bounded up the stairs with pulsars ready. The sight he saw in the candlelight he would never forget. Nick was lying on his back in the bed, his face bloated and swollen almost beyond recognition. And there, beside him, were Tara and an old man who was trying to force something between Nick's clenched teeth. "Stop!" he yelled. "What are you doing to him?" He resisted an impulse to kill them on the spot. The old man was startled. Tara quickly stood up. In the half-light, she saw the two pulsars trained on her. She saw the menace in Matt's eyes and gestured helplessly toward Nick lying unconscious in the bed. She silently appealed to Matt with her eyes, telling him, "Nick is terribly sick. Can you help him?"

Matt studied her and understood. He saw her haggard appearance and the worried look in her eyes. He realized that she had been up with Nick all night. For a moment, he sensed her sorrow, and he had an impulse to comfort her. Then, abruptly, he remembered his resolve not to allow himself to be manipulated by the all too human appearing aliens. He turned from her and focused on Nick's swollen face. Training his pulsars on the two of them, he gestured threateningly for them to back themselves out through the other door. As they exited, he closed it then bent down and managed to hoist Nick's limp body over his shoulder.

Still holding a pulsar in his left hand, he was able to get down the stairs and through the house. Not seeing anyone, he opened the outside door and then stumbled down the two steps leading from the porch. Getting up off his knees, he made it to the amcar and was able to get Nick's limp body inside. Lurching forward, he turned the car and headed toward the space module. A huge winged bird flew across his path as he accelerated into overdrive.

Almost immediately he was flying high over the treetops. Suddenly he saw another enormous creature diving toward him on a collision course. He maneuvered his craft wildly, somehow managing to avoid impact. "Whew! That was close," he exclaimed. He sat tensely at the controls, wondering what else they might unleash against him.

The rest of the short trip back to the ship was uneventful. He took the precaution of circling the module a few times and could see no sign that anything had disturbed the area. He landed near the entrance, stepped out with pulsars drawn, and entered the ship. Everything appeared to be normal.

Going back to the amcar, he lifted Nick out, dragged him inside, and laid him on his bed. Nick didn't look good. His face remained so swollen that he probably couldn't have opened his eyes if he wanted to. On further examination, he didn't appear to be bruised or have any broken limbs. Opening the medical kit, Matt took a sample of Nick's blood and put it into the bioanalyzer. The results took longer than normal to read out. They showed an extremely high white blood cell count caused by the invasion of an unknown bacterial strain. Matt punched its genetic code into the analyzer for an antibody and waited. He waited for what seemed like a long time. Finally the answer came. There was none. The type of bacteria infecting Nick had never before been encountered.

Matt took a deep breath. Suddenly he felt very tired. Although he had done all he could for Nick, the lack of a remedy could prove fatal. Frustrated, he fixed himself a drink and said a prayer. He lay down, and after awhile, fell into a fitful sleep.

Several hours later, he was wakened by the perimeter alarms. Jumping out of bed, he reached for his pulsar and looked out the window. It was Tara. She was approaching the entrance. Looking up, she saw him at the window. He pointed the pulsar at her and motioned her to go back. She lowered her head, ignoring the threat, and continued forward until she stood beneath the window. She looked up into his eyes, and he returned her gaze, looking at her closely for the first time. She was a slender young woman who seemed sad and tired, hardly anyone to be feared. He sensed that she was terribly concerned about Nick. He struggled within himself, trying hard not to show any compassion toward her. Feeling rather insensitive, he turned away and closed the window shade.

Time passed. Bridestar's yellowish orange sun rose high in the sky.

"Oh, God! Oh, my head!" Nick cried out, in intense pain.

Matt got up from the chair where he had been catnapping and rushed over to him. Nicked moaned, holding his head in his hands, as he twisted in agony. "Help me Matt. Please help me."

Matt hurried over to the dispensary, fumbled for a painkiller, and returning to Nick, pressed the nozzle into the base of his neck. For awhile longer, Nick writhed in agony until gradually the medication began working. Then, he lay quiet and unmoving.

Matt paced back and forth in the cabin, not knowing what else to do for him. Eventually, Nick wakened. Lifting his head he asked, "What happened to me?"

Matt approached the side of the bed. "Glad you're better, Nick. Last night, when I brought you back here, your face was so swollen, you couldn't have talked if you wanted to. Do you have any memory of that?"

"No. I don't. The last thing I remember, I was walking away from Tara's house, and then I lost control of my legs and fell down. I don't remember anything after that until I woke up here."

"How do you feel now?"

"Like I've been drugged, and I'm just coming out of it. Extremely tired."

"No wonder. When I found you last night you were in a bed at her house. You looked like you were dying. In fact, I didn't know if you would survive. I'll tell you more about all that later, but for now, you need to get some more rest. Do you want anything to eat?"

"No, thanks."

"Here, I'll give you another dose of the pain killer. Hopefully when you wake up again you'll feel better."

A few hours later, Nick again opened his eyes. This time he felt OK. His headache was gone, and he had an appetite. He tried moving his legs. Although his body felt rigid, he was able to roll out of bed, get up on his feet, and walk stiffly over to the food synthesizer. Noticing that the window was dark, he deactivated the shade to let in more light. Then he saw Tara. She was bent over, lying against the side of the landing gear. He opened the door and gingerly stepped down. She lifted her head at his approach and smiled at him. He stiffly extended his hand to help her up.

"How long have you been here?"

"Since morning."

"Really? Why didn't you come in?"

"I think Matt was afraid to open the door."

"Why? That doesn't make sense. Why would he do that?"

She proceeded to tell him about what happened after he fell down on the road. How Matt had come early in the morning to "rescue" him. "I believe he thinks I poisoned you," she concluded.

"Damn! What's with him? Why can't he forget those paranoid ideas of his?" He took her hand, and walking directly into the module, he confronted Matt.

Nick began sarcastically. "Thanks for saving me from Tara. Do you know she's been waiting outside all day because you wouldn't let her in?"

"I'm sorry Nick. I was afraid you'd been poisoned, and I didn't. . ."

Just then, the perimeter alarm sounded. Looking out the window, Nick saw Tara's grandfather dismounting from his forc. Walking cautiously to the ship, he knocked on the door.

Nick opened it, saying, "Come in."

The older man looked past him. "Tara!" he said with relief. "We've been looking all over for you." Then he focused on Matt and Nick. Turning to Nick, he said, "I'm glad to see you've recovered, young man."

"Thanks. I still feel weak, but I'm glad to be alive after last night. Mr. Ruskin, this is my friend and partner, Matt." The two reluctantly shook hands. Nick could see that Ruskin was uncomfortable in Matt's presence.

"I won't hurt you," Matt said. He looked at Ruskin to see if he comprehended what he said. "I know I imagined the worst, especially when I saw Nick's face so badly swollen."

Ruskin nodded. "You think of us as different, Matt, but if you get to know us you'll find we're just as sentient as you are." He turned to face them all. "It just occurred to me that Nick's sudden sickness must have been caused by an allergic reaction to something in the food he ate at our house."

Nick looked to Tara, verifying what he thought Ruskin said. "That sounds plausible," he answered. "A delayed reaction. Probably something you have a natural immunity for that we haven't acquired."

"If we can isolate the substance we can analyze it and possibly develop an antidote," Matt added. "If not, we will definitely avoid it."

"Then all we need to do is find out everything Shari used in yesterday's dinner," declared Tara.

"Yes, if we bring it here, we can isolate it in the bioanalyzer and see if it reacts with samples of Nick's blood."

"Can you really do it that simply?" asked Ruskin.

"Oh, yes," Matt replied, finding that he was able to decipher more of the conversation himself. "The equipment we have on board will do a lot, though it's not like having a complete laboratory. It should be able to show us the causative element."

Although Ruskin was in awe at the advanced technology, he tried not to show it. "If it's that easy," he said, "let's get to it. I brought your forc, Tara. We can talk to Shari, get samples of everything, and come back here in the morning."

Tara looked at Nick, then turned back to her grandfather. "Yes, I guess we should leave before dark, especially at this time of year."

Nick moved to be next to her and said, "I'll look forward to seeing you tomorrow." Then she and Ruskin were off, riding with surprising swiftness.

The next day dawned bright and clear with a slight chill in the air. Nick waved when he saw Tara and Ruskin returning.

"How do you feel today?" asked Tara, her eyes expressing concern.

"Just fine," he replied. "I'm loose and limber and ready for anything today." He flexed his arms to demonstrate.

Tara laughed and said, "I don't think anything could keep you down for long."

"You're probably right. By the way, is that some of the native fare that you're bringing for us to eat today?"

"Yes, that's what it is," she replied, catching the spirit of his banter. "We feel it's our duty to share with the less fortunate."

"Well, thank you kindly, miss." He took the small, wrapped package from her and added. "I'll tell my partner that the natives here seem to be friendly. Hey Matt, here's the food samples."

"OK., bring them in. I've got the analyzer set up."

"Could I see how it works?" asked Ruskin.

"Sure. Go right in," replied Nick. "And take these samples in with you. Matt can show you how the tests are run."

Tara backed up to let her grandfather by and found herself captured in Nick's arms. She looked up over her shoulder at him. "Is this the way spacemen treat girls on other planets?" she said coquettishly.

"Of course. We try to make a lasting impression with all the girls. That way when we come back, we're always welcome. Matt and I have girls on all the planets we've been to, Yaltum, Bircolae, Shantun, and Firesta."

"Really?" She slipped out of his arms and turned to face him. Seeing his smile, she said, "I don't believe it." But she didn't know for sure and stepped out of his reach when he tried to hold her again.

"I was only kidding," Nick said. "Didn't you know that?"

Tara looked up at him, her eyes flashing a mixture of hurt and relief. "Well, it's not the way to talk to someone you care about."

Just then, the ship's door opened and Ruskin stepped out. "All findings are negative so far, but I have an idea. Tara, would you join us inside for a minute? I have a hunch I'd like to check out."

"Sure. I'm glad to help any way I can." Still sulking, she walked past Nick without a glance and stepped inside. Within ten minutes, she came back out. Matt and Ruskin appeared at the door. Both of them were smiling. Tara walked over to Nick, looked him straight in the eyes and said, "I'm afraid what you're allergic to is me."

"I don't believe it," Nick exclaimed. He thought a moment. "That kiss on the trail, before we parted?"

"I'm afraid that was it," she said. "I'm so sorry. I didn't mean to hurt you."

"Hurting isn't what concerns me now," he said, drawing her close. "I was just getting to know you," he said softly so the others couldn't hear him. "I don't want that to end."

"I know, Nick," she replied, barely audible, as she nestled in his arms. "I don't want it to end either."

"There has to be a way to overcome this, and we're going to find it."

"Yes, she agreed, taking heart. My grandfather may be able to help. He knows a lot about herbal medicine. I think he can find a cure."

Matt said, "I can go through the computer's medical journals. Maybe we can develop a vaccine."

Then for a short time no one said anything. Tara broke the silence. "I need to get back to the center. They've been backing me up, but I need to return to work now. She faced Nick squarely, her countenance expressing the sadness she felt. Though she didn't speak, Nick read her concern. Was she going to lose him now? Did it really mean enough to him to try? What if finding a cure was difficult? What if there was no cure? She looked at him steadily and then stepped forward to give him a parting hug. "Please be careful. The month of Ravidian has started. Watch out for the Thorns, especially early in the morning and just after sunset. Promise me you'll be careful."

Nick said he would take precautions, and Tara and Ruskin said goodbye and rode away,

Love Strokes

leaving only the paw marks of their mounts. Nick felt dejected. He looked out at the savanna in front of him then turned and stepped back into the ship. He was tired. Matt had already left to go somewhere with the car. Nick got a glass of water and sat down to think. Why did he feel the way he did? There were lots of girls in the galaxy. He had always believed that. Why was this one affecting him so much? Certainly there wasn't anyone like her. But then again, how well did he really know her? His thoughts were disorganized. Finally, he went to the computer, selected an old movie, sat in front of the EV, and waited for Matt to return.

After the short film ended, Nick looked outside and saw Matt getting out of the amcar.

"Where'd you go?" he asked, opening the door.

"Nick, I just got back from taking another look at sector 38. I thought it might be worth further testing, so I took the equipment over there. I made some inferences based on our earlier samples and sent the probe down. When I sent it down this time, I had a hunch it might be the right spot. Look." He lifted the probe onto the table and pointed out the oily film clinging to its sides.

"Oh, yes. Yes!" Nick exclaimed. "You found it!" The two of them whooped, high fived, and punched each other in their excitement. When their fervor subsided a bit, Matt fingered the lock to open catch door number seven of the automatic probe. As the door opened, thick, black oil oozed out.

"Whoa! That's what we've been looking for," said Nick. He collected some in a small vial and lifted it to his nose. "Mm, I like that smell. Were you able to find out if it's very extensive?"

"Not yet. The field doesn't appear to rise very high, but it could run deep. As for area, I don't know yet."

During supper they speculated extensively on how much oil they might find and planned the locations where they would sink the next probes. It was particularly exciting work for Matt, who had never been involved in a find. Nick had helped discover an oil site once before, but it had unfortunately been deemed "Not economically feasible to remove, using current technology." Still, he knew that this time could very well be different, and with a major discovery, they would quickly become wealthy and famous. The excitement stimulated them, and they worked far into the night planning for the next day.

In the morning after a hasty breakfast, they were back in the car, heading for their first site. As they approached it, they saw two huge birds take wing. Matt whistled in amazement. "Look at the size of those creatures!

"No wonder the townspeople are afraid of them. Their beaks must be almost a yard long."

Nick guided the car down to the site. The Thorns, however, instead of flying off as expected, began a wide turn at low altitude around the amcar.

Nick pointed south. "Look. They haven't left. See them over the treetops there?"

"They look like they're circling us."

"Obviously we didn't scare them off."

"Maybe we had better wait in the car for awhile. Tara said they will attack people at this time of year."

They stayed inside for another half-hour until the birds flew out of sight. When they left the ship they remained on high alert, pulsars ready, in case they returned. Not seeing any more of them, they went back to drilling and found an abundance of oil. Almost every time they sank the probe into the ground, it returned holding more of the precious black crude.

As the evening sun was setting on the horizon, they finished packing and congratulated themselves as they headed back to the ship.

"What a day!" exclaimed Matt, wiping his brow. "This is the stuff of dreams."

"Like a special fishing spot where you catch a big one every time you cast," Nick agreed.

"I can't wait to get all this data into the computer so we can see the whole picture."

"Right. We definitely have quite a concentration. How extensive it is we will soon find out."

When they returned to the ship, they didn't even think about eating. Quickly finishing the graphs, they entered the data and let the computer make the analyses. They didn't have long to wait.

"Look at this," said Matt, practically pulling the analagram from the printer. "We've got major concentrations in all the areas surrounding sector 38."

"Yes," Nick concurred, as he stood up to examine the analagram. "But notice, Matt, how it begins to thin out as we move further along the edges."

"Like a deep lake with a shallow shoreline."

Love Strokes

"I hope that's not what we're seeing here. I saw that on Bircolae. A pocket of oil hemmed in by a range of nonporous rock."

"So, in other words, we've got oil but we still don't know if it's worthwhile?"

"It's worth something. We just don't know yet if there's enough to come this far to extract."

The perimeter alarm sounded, and within moments, they heard sharp knocking on the door. "Tara," said Nick, as he opened the door. "What's the matter?"

She quickly came inside, obviously very upset. "The Thorns," she uttered between breaths. "They killed Petra! It was horrible! She stopped again to breathe. "One of those, those. . .creatures, tried to carry him back. He was still alive and struggling. It was taking him away, but he fought it and fell from its grasp. We found his body in the woods. His neck was broken." She bowed her head and sobbed.

Nick moved to her and held her close. He didn't know what to say, but he held her until she stopped shaking. She looked up at him, and returning his embrace, put her head on his chest and closed her eyes tightly, as if trying to block out the memory of what she had seen.

"I'm sorry, Tara," Nick spoke softly. "Was he one of yours?"

She nodded, lifting her head. "One of the best." Again, the tears welled up in her eyes.

"If there's anything we can do to help, we will," he said.

Matt seconded him, "Yes, we would like to do something."

Tara looked at them and said gratefully, "Thank you so much. You could come to the funeral. I would appreciate that. That is, if you have time."

"Of course," Nick answered. "When is it?"

"Normally it's done at night, but during this month everything is done during the day because of the Thorns. It will be tomorrow afternoon."

The wake was held at the youth's house. All the family, relatives, and most of the neighbors attended. In fact, it was hard to get in. Nick and Matt had not planned to stay long. While there, they met a number of the townspeople, many of whom seemed curious about them. Some even asked who they were and what they were doing. Tara helped with introductions whenever she was nearby. Nick caught parts of conversations, and sensed that the majority of people there were quite concerned and worried about the Thorns. Already, a house-to-house sentry program had been started. If one of the creatures was seen, sentries would ring a warning bell, so everyone would know to run home or to the nearest shelter. Nick learned that people stayed inside at night, making only the most furtive trips from one house to another, and then, only if it was necessary.

The fear was tangible. What was even worse, from Nick's perspective, was the general perception that it would be foolhardy to fight back. He learned that many of the townspeople believed that if they did manage to kill one of the creatures, the whole colony would attack in force. Matt heard the same thing, and when they had a moment to discuss it between themselves, they both felt that it was an irrational fear. At one point, Matt, who was becoming irritated by all the fearful talk, told one of the guests that if a Thorn came close to him, he would shoot it out of the sky. He was apparently understood well enough, because word began circulating that they had lethal weapons.

As they were getting ready to leave, they learned that those who came for the wake were also expected to attend the funeral, which had been scheduled for the next morning. Tara had already made accommodation for them at her house, and it was only after much discourse that Nick was able to convince her that it would be safe for them to return overnight to the ship.

Actually, Nick would have stayed, but he knew that Matt was anxious to return to the comfort and security of the space module. Nick appreciated that Matt had given up his time to come to the wake and that he was willing to go to the funeral tomorrow. So, after saying goodbye and receiving insistent admonitions to be careful, they walked back to the amcar. After all the talk, they were tense as they pulled away from the town, quickly reaching cruising speed above the treetops. Soon they were back at the module, where they felt safe in their familiar surroundings.

The next morning dawned bright with thin hazy clouds. Matt agreed to go to the funeral only if they left immediately afterwards. They were both anxious to get back to the oil fields. As they prepared to leave, Nick looked out the window and saw one of the huge flying creatures. This time, it was much closer. "We have company," he whispered, as if the bird could hear through the insulation of the ship.

"Look at the size of it," Matt replied, in a hushed voice. The creature was on the ground, less than one hundred yards away.

Partially hidden by a low tree, it appeared to stand about fifteen feet tall. Through the branches, they could see its eyes. It appeared to be stalking them.

"This one is going to be in for a surprise," whispered Nick, as he got out his pulsar and charged it to full strength. Matt did the same. They stepped outside. The Thorn immediately spread its huge wings and climbed into the air. Rapidly it bridged the distance between them, its murderous pointed beak aimed right at them. A low hum emitted from the two pulsars. The bird crashed to the ground, dead, forty feet in front of them. Another one, apparently its partner, emerged from behind the ship and flew swiftly away over the treetops. Matt walked over and kicked the dead body, saying, "This dumb bird won't bother anyone again."

At the funeral service, they sat with Tara, Ruskin, Shari, and her daughter. Before the opening hymn, Nick mentioned to them that they had killed one of the birds. Ruskin was aghast.

"Don't you realize that if you kill one, the whole colony will return to avenge their dead?" He continued to talk, in a very agitated manner, asking them more questions about the incident. Tara, too, appeared to be frightened for them, but she was able to calm herself, and even her grandfather, before the service started.

After the ceremony, both Ruskin and Tara spoke with Nick and Matt about the consequences of killing a Thorn. When they learned that there was a second one that got away, they were even more appalled. It was not long before the news reached the people who remained after the service, and soon everyone was talking about it. Tara insisted that Nick and Matt not go back to the ship. Others informed them that there could be thousands of Thorns nested in their rocky cliff dwellings, many miles away.

Nick and Matt were definitely going to return to the space module. They were more concerned about the need to protect it from damage than anything else. Breaking away from their well-meaning friends, they returned to the amcar and headed back.

"What do you think?" asked Nick, as he guided the vehicle over the trees. "Do you think the Thorns will come back?"

"I doubt it. Maybe it *has* happened before, but my impression is that it must have been in the distant past, if at all. I have to admit though, they were all certainly scared."

"Yes, that was evident. I agree with your analysis. The retaliation story may be a legend that's been handed down for generations. They're so afraid of the creatures to begin with, something like that could be blown way out of proportion."

"Still, if there's any truth at all to it, I want to be prepared. That ship is our trip home."

Back at the star module, they went to work cutting down some small trees. Their plan was to make a barrier of scaffolding around the ship using poles spaced several feet apart and tied together at right angles. That way, none of the birds would be able to get through to land on the ship. They were hard at work, sawing logs the old fashioned way, to conserve pulsar power, when they were surprised to see people approaching. The visitors came in pairs, riding forcs, each two carrying a long log between their mounts. Among the early arrivals were Tara and Ruskin. Tara dismounted, walked toward Nick and said, "They all wanted to help, Nick."

Nick looked past her to see Ruskin in the background, already directing the positioning of the poles. "You really do think they're going to attack, don't you, Tara." He put down his saw and hugged her.

He noted the concern and fear in her eyes. "You don't have to worry, Tara. We're going to be all right. See this." He withdrew his pulsar and showed it to her. "This is instant death for those creatures. If they dare to come close, they'll regret it."

She placed her hand on top of the pulsar, felt the hard molded polymer, and sensed the power of it. "Do you have any more of these?" she asked.

"Yes, we each have a spare."

"Is it hard to use?"

"Not at all," he answered, beginning to discern where the conversation was leading.

"Then I want to stay with you to help when they attack."

"No, Tara. I appreciate your wanting to help. If they do come back, this could be a very dangerous place to be. You know I care about you. I sure don't want to take a chance that you could be hurt. Besides, if it happens, it's our battle."

"It's our battle too, Nick," she insisted, her eyes flashing. "It was one of us who was killed by those creatures. It was my neighbor's son who died. We are the ones who have to live in fear of them. Don't you see? The battle may be fought at your ship, but it will be fought on our soil. We are the ones who win if the Thorns are killed."

Nick couldn't dispute her logic, as much as he wanted to. "OK," he replied, putting his hand on her shoulder. "If you feel that strongly about it, you can stay with us. We will prepare for combat. I will teach you how to shoot this, and if they come, you can shoot them out of the sky. Is that what you want to do?"

Tara nodded and looked up at him, tears glistening in her eyes, but smiling at the same time.

"What are you crying about?" Nick asked, mystified.

"I don't know. I guess I'm just happy to be here with you. I wish I could kiss you."

"Yes, that is a problem," he acknowledged. "I've been thinking about that and have an idea about how it can be solved."

"Really?" she asked, enthusiastically.

"Well, it's a process that might take awhile. I'll tell you about it when we have more time."

"Great! I would like to show you how we in Crystal kiss."

"Sounds interesting. I'll definitely have to show you how North Amis kiss.

"Hi, Tara," said Matt. "Nick, can you give me a hand with this log?"

The work of building the fortifications proceeded. Most of the long poles the townspeople had brought were now in place, and viewing them from the spaceship, Nick and Matt could see how the tall posts would prevent the Thorns, with their long wingspans, from getting through. The two of them, along with Tara continued work on building the smaller structure of logs and branches surrounding the module. As evening approached, they stood back and surveyed the battlements. Around them for forty yards in every direction, stood poles about five inches thick, thirty feet high and twelve feet apart. Across the ship itself, struts were positioned about six feet apart, with a patchwork of thick branches tied five feet above the top of the ship.

"I think we're about done," said Ruskin. He walked over to say a few words to the last of the townspeople who had finished erecting a pole. Then he walked back to the ship.

"Thanks so much for all your help," said Nick. "I'm still hoping we won't need all this."

"You're perfectly welcome," answered Ruskin. You know we're all pulling for you boys. You will do us a real favor if you can kill some of those horrid creatures. My prayer is that all these posts will keep them from getting through to you."

"They should certainly help," Matt replied.

"Tara, we had better be leaving, before it gets too late," Ruskin said.

"I'm staying here tonight, grandpa."

Ruskin looked surprised but didn't answer. Instead, his eyes locked steadily on hers. Finally, he turned and said to all of them, "I'm staying here too. Do you have an extra cot for an old man? And, an extra pulsar?"

That evening they practiced using the pulsars. Tara quickly learned to shoot with remarkable accuracy. Ruskin had a harder time getting used to the handgun; though with practice, he too, was able to do OK.

None of the Thorns appeared while they were practicing, and as darkness fell without a sign of them, they began to feel more relaxed. Nick ordered some delicious food from the restant, and after eating an excellent supper, they thought that if the Thorns didn't come, they might as well enjoy the evening together. First, however, they spent time working on strategy, in order to be prepared for any eventualities. Tara quickly grew tired of that. She went to the other side of the cabin and leaned back in a chair, obviously bored.

After awhile, Nick noticed her there. He

got up, turned on some music, and asked her to dance. She smiled, stood up, and was quickly in his arms. He turned up the volume and held her close. It was surprising to him how well she followed his lead. Then, faster paced music began playing, and they separated. For a minute, she watched him dance alone. Then she joined him. Nick laughed as she tried to follow his movements, adding her own variations. She smiled when she looked up and saw Ruskin and Matt watching her.

On the next song Matt joined them and, after a warm-up, started his inimitable fast step style. Nick sat down and saw Tara attempt to follow Matt. She couldn't keep up with him, and started to laugh. At first, she tried to hide it by putting her hand over her mouth, but she couldn't keep it in. Matt hardly noticed, he was so much into the music.

When the song ended, Nick and Ruskin applauded them. Matt theatrically bowed and then took Tara in his arms as a slower melody began. Matt was a good dancer, Nick had to admit, as he and Tara swirled around the cabin. He glanced at Ruskin who was watching them dance with what looked like amused contentment. Nick and Matt continued dancing a while longer, taking turns with Tara.

Eventually, Ruskin stood up and told them he was ready to go to bed. They all thought it was a good idea as it was already getting late and they didn't know what tomorrow would bring. Matt offered his bed to Ruskin, who insisted on taking the cot instead. Nick offered his to Tara, who tried lying on it and remarked how comfortable it was. Nick prepared for bed, and when he returned to the sleeping quarters, he found Tara already under the blankets. For a moment, he forgot and started to kiss her goodnight, until they both remembered at the same time and instead hugged briefly.

As he started to leave, Tara looked up at him and said, "When I was a little girl my mother would tuck me in and kiss me goodnight. Then my father would come in and give me a big hug before blowing out the candle. Since they died, I've missed that, but somehow you make me feel cared for like they did."

"I don't know exactly why," he said, "but I'm very comfortable with you, too. I feel that you're genuine and unpretentious, and it pleases me that you're so open to try new things. Like the dance steps you picked up so quickly tonight. And more important, how you seem to have accepted me, a stranger from a world you know so little about."

She patted the bed, inviting him to sit down. "I know what you're saying. From the first time I saw you, I sensed a gentleness in you that makes me feel special. I feel I can trust you, and it makes me lose my reserve.

Nick looked into her eyes, and stroked the inside of her arm. He smiled down at her. Squeezing her hand in his, he got up, saying, "I hope we get to know each other very well." He gently blew her a kiss and turned off the light.

Chapter Four

In the morning, they woke to see the birds—not as many as they feared, just a few circling above languidly. Nick speculated that they were surveying the fortifications.

"These few will give us no trouble," stated Matt, who seemed anxious to begin the fray.

"Maybe they'll just go, and leave us alone," Tara said, hopefully.

"I hope you're right," Nick replied. "Just so they're not the scouting party."

"Unfortunately, that's a distinct possibility," said Ruskin.

As they watched, their fears were realized. Advancing from the west, a rapidly moving dark cloud appeared. As it came closer, they could see that it was made up of a multitude of flapping wings.

"Look at that!" said Nick in awe.

They watched in horror as the huge cloud approached until the birds were directly above them, circling, screeching, and making short dives in their direction. Without speaking, Tara turned to look at Nick. Nick looked back at her and then at Matt and at Ruskin. Wordlessly they resolved that, whatever the odds, they would stand and fight.

Nick and Matt spoke briefly with each other. They were concerned that the perimeter shields might use up too much energy trying to withstand such a massive onslaught. As they conferred, a Thorn crashed into the shield, and then another and another. Although individual Thorns were stopped by it, the rest didn't stop coming. A check of the energy monitors showed that the system was approaching overload. "I'm shutting down the perimeter shield," announced Nick. "Ready your pulsars."

"Look!" yelled Tara, pointing out the window. "They're landing over there by the poles." The men left their positions at the other windows to watch the huge birds alighting on the ground just outside the line of defense. There were seven of them, and as they watched from inside the ship, the creatures began attacking the shafts with their powerful beaks.

"I don't think those poles can withstand that long," Ruskin asserted. Already they could see splinters flying under the attack. Then, the first pole went down.

"We shouldn't wait any longer," Matt declared.

"No," answered Nick. "Let's get them!" He slid the window open. The pulsars hummed their lethal power, and four of the Thorns dropped. Two were completely motionless while the other two still quivered. The others started to take flight, and one was hit in mid air, falling with a thud to the ground.

Overcoming the immediate threat, they were elated, until they looked out the window on the other side. Massed there were at least a dozen more of them. They had already started to attack the outer poles, and the wood was breaking apart. Two of the logs crashed to the ground. As the pulsars discharged again, more Thorns fell sprawling to their deaths. Nevertheless, huge numbers of them continued to land around the outer poles. Now they were coming from every direction.

Though the birds were easy targets, they began coming in so fast that they were able to break down the shafts before they could be killed. The defenders soon became aware of another concern. They weren't able to recharge the guns fast enough, even though Tara was now working the charger full time. If the onslaught continued, it would only be a matter of time before they would be landing outside the doors. The bodies of the fallen Thorns were heaping up along the outer logs, but those that had not been shot hopped over the dead ones and continued battering the posts. It was strange, Nick thought, that they kept coming, as if programmed. Even imminent death didn't deter them. The poles kept crashing down.

Abruptly, the noise stopped. As they watched, the Thorns on the ground stretched their wings and rose up to join the ones still circling above. Then only the flapping of wings was heard as the whole assemblage began moving away from the ship. One bird, larger and blacker than the others, flew high in front of the rest, seeming to lead the way. The huge cloud passed over them and moved back to the west. In a few minutes, they were out of sight.

"I do hope they've given up," voiced Tara.

It was a sentiment they all felt. Around the outer area of the fortifications stood the remnants of shattered poles and the bodies of lifeless birds. They covered an area forty or more feet wide and up to ten feet high. Though it was a horrible sight, somehow the defenders couldn't take their eyes off it. At last, they looked away from the carnage and realized how hungry they were. It was already nearing noon, and they hadn't eaten anything. Tara, with Nick's help, made lunch. As they sat tired and quiet at the table, they silently gave thanks for their survival. Not one of them believed that the Thorns wouldn't return.

Ruskin left the main room to take a nap, and Nick and Matt went outside to look at the full extent of the damage. They wanted to see what repairs could be made to the fortifications. Tara stayed inside for awhile and then came out. However, the sight and the smell of all the dead birds repulsed her, and she soon went back in.

She looked at the cabin, trying to imagine what it would be like to live there for a two-month space trip. She glanced out the window and saw Nick and Matt alongside one of the poles, tying on a crossbeam for added protection. Out of the corner of her eye, she caught sight of something moving in the sky. In a moment she knew what it was. She hastened to open the door and call out to Nick and Matt. The Thorns were back.

By the time they were all inside the cabin, the creatures were already closing in, and rising high above the others was the great lead Thorn. As they watched, it turned to one side, appearing to look down on them. Although it was still far up in the sky, Nick had the distinct impression that its eyes were red. He pointed it out to Matt.

"See that one there, above all the rest? If it comes in range, let's try to knock it down." Their view of it was almost immediately obscured however, as the Thorns started circling in a huge black cloud directly above the ship. They readied their pulsars in preparation for another attack on the remaining poles. But it didn't come, and the Thorns continued to fly in a large circle above the ship. They waited, wondering what would happen next.

As they watched, a bird dropped out of the sky toward the ship.

"Shoot!" yelled Nick, touching open the window. The Thorn's head went limp, but its body hurtled toward them like a rock. It landed a few feet from the ship with a loud thud, shattering a pole as it fell.

"That was close." Matt yelled. A second bird dropped from the sky. "Get it!" he shouted. It was on Ruskin's side, and he shot three times before it folded and dropped its head. The creature's dead body fell like a brick, landing inches from the ship.

"I'm going outside!" shouted Nick. "We've got to hit them immediately when they start their dive or it's going to be too late."

When the Thorns saw Nick, they went into a frenzy, diving toward him rather than at the ship. Like bombs, they began dropping from the sky. Nick held on to his pulsar with both hands, firing at the fiendish creatures diving at him from out of the swirling maelstrom. He pivoted around in a circle, trying to keep ahead of the Thorns coming down at him from every direction. As his pulsar found its targets, their heads drooped, their wings folded, and they fell, sometimes knocking down logs as they crashed to the ground.

"Look out!" shouted Tara. Nick spun around, firing a late shot at one that came from behind. The bird died a quick death, but its body snapped a pole, which landed on Nick's thigh. He fell down. Tara gasped, and Matt sprinted from the cabin, firing as the Thorns continued to dive bomb them. Nick pushed the log off his leg, got up, and the two of them, standing back to back, fired at the unrelenting Thorns. Nick yelled to Tara that his pulsar power was weakening. She threw him a recharged one, and he tossed the spent one back to her.

The battle continued. It went on for a long time, until the whole area was littered with shattered poles and dead Thorns. There didn't appear to be any end to them. Then, as if by signal, the screeching stopped. In silence, they continued to circle above, until, as if called by a mysterious signal, they again began moving to the west. Despite all the birds left on the ground, the number above seemed only slightly diminished. As they flew off, Nick could once again see the large black bird flying above all the rest, leading them home.

The four of them were exhausted, not only by the activity, but also by all the tension they had been under. Words were few. Tara wanted Nick to lie down so that she could look at his injured thigh. She was glad to see that although it was dark and swollen, there were no open wounds or lacerations. Matt went to the restant to order a meal, which they ate stoically. The pulsars were again recharged up to their maximum.

They went about their few activities woodenly. Around the ship, the view was desolate. Thorn bodies were everywhere among the splintered logs, and a few were impaled on the poles. Despite the scene of overall destruction, the logs and bracketing immediately surrounding the ship remained intact. By virtue of Nick and Matt's skillful shooting and luck, none of the creatures had landed on the framework. That structure remained, their last line of defense. How much longer would it hold? The unspoken question was on all of their minds. Nick and Matt went outside to add some bracing to reinforce it. As darkness fell, they returned inside to join Ruskin and Tara.

Tara was talking to Ruskin at the table. She looked up as they entered and asked, "How does it look?"

"Not bad, considering," Nick answered. "Our main barrier around the ship is intact, and we added some timber to make it stronger."

"Can I fix you both something to drink?"

"Not for me, thanks," Matt replied. "I just want to lie down."

"I'd have a cup of chocolate with you," Nick answered.

"No thanks for me," said Ruskin. "I'm going to bed too."

Tara went to the restant to order the chocolate. She came back to the table with two cups of the piping hot brew. She studied Nick for a moment and set the cups on the table. She could see his weariness.

"You should go to bed too, Nick. You've been working so hard out there."

"I know," he said, reaching for her hand across the table. "They just don't seem to want to give up. This whole thing is a terrible nightmare."

"Yes," she said, caressing his hand. "I know you and Matt have been doing all you can. You need to rest now. Try to put it out of your mind for awhile."

"I wish I could."

She got up and, bending down, hugged him around the neck. "You're so tense. Let me give you a massage. Turn your back to me." As she worked with firm hands on his tightened neck and back muscles, Nick could feel some of the tension leaving his body.

"Thank you. That feels much better."

They parted to go to their beds, and after a short time, all four of them were asleep. But the Thorns fought on in their dreams, as they had during the day.

Long before daybreak, Nick woke up. He thought he heard something coming from above. Listening attentively, he was sure of it. A look out the window confirmed his worst fears. Without touching on any of the lights, he roused the others. They gathered together in the darkness. Then they heard loud scratching sounds overhead. Nick stood on a chair to open the hatch in order to see what was going on. What he saw made his hair stand on end. The creatures were landing on the bracketing, scarcely six feet above him.

"Matt. Hurry! They're piling up on top of the framework. With all their weight they're going to break it down!"

He and Matt began firing through the hatch into the massing bodies. The blood of the wounded birds drained down through the opening, drenching them. Ruskin grabbed his pulsar and a chair and joined them while Tara returned to the job of recharging the pulsars. So much blood was streaming down, that all three of the men soon looked like they were mortally wounded. Outside, the carcasses were piling up around the module, as they fell from the top. Then they heard a sharp crack, followed immediately by loud pounding that rocked the ship. The birds had broken through the barrier. They were swarming on top the module!

Inside, they could hear beaks pecking and claws scratching, trying to force a way in. Nick glanced at Matt and then rushed out the door, slamming it behind him. He clambered over the bodies and began shooting at the horde that was still coming down from the sky and landing on the ship. Intent on the module, they didn't at first notice him. Nick began to feel a sense of hopelessness as he realized that there were just too many of them. If the attack continued, they would burst through long before they could all be killed. He had an idea. His eyes searched the sky high above him, hoping to glimpse in the pale moonlight the huge black Thorn with the red eyes.

It was no use. There were just too many of them flying about, blocking his view. There was a clearing, and peering through it, Nick recognized the huge Thorn, still flying high above the others. He steadied his hands and fired carefully, once, twice, three times. On the third shot, he thought he saw the creature shudder, but his view was again obscured.

He continued to watch for several more seconds. Again, there was another clearing, but it showed nothing of the huge Thorn he was looking for. Had he shot it down? And, if so, did it make any difference at all? Apparently not, he decided, as the Thorns continued unabated their onslaught against the ship. He fired repeatedly at the Thorns landing there, but his pulsar was beginning to lose power. He heard Tara scream at him through the open door of the module, and he turned to see a gigantic Thorn with blood red eyes bearing down on him. He tried to jump out of its path, but was knocked to the ground. He felt the sharp stab of its beak in his left side.

Suddenly he felt extremely weak and thirsty, and he realized he was in danger of passing out. Managing somehow to deal with the pain, he tightened his grip on the pulsar. Then he saw Tara climbing up over the dead Thorns as she rushed toward him. "Go back," he tried to shout, but in his weakened condition, his voice sounded feeble, even to himself. She kept on coming.

He saw the Thorn returning to finish him off. As the creature zeroed in on him, he raised his pulsar for one last shot. At the last moment, the giant bird saw Tara and altered its course. Nick saw it turn toward her. As it closed in on her, he fired once and then again. His pulsar was spent, but the bird's terrible eyes closed, and its body trembled. Its momentum carried it forward, and it crashed to the ground between Nick and Tara, covering them with its still outstretched wings. It didn't move.

"Nick!" screamed Tara. "Are you alright?"

"Yes," he lied. "Are you OK?"

"Yes," he heard her answer.

Then, from underneath the outstretched wings of the Thorn, came a sound like heavy drops of rain. Next, from the direction of the ship he heard yelling. It sounded like cheering. *Why would they be cheering?* Nick wondered dimly as he lapsed into unconsciousness.

Chapter Five

The first thing Nick saw was Tara bending over his bed. She was attending to the wound on his left side and looked so anxious that he smiled weakly at her and said, "Surely it can't be that bad."

"Nick," she cried, the sadness immediately leaving her face. "You were badly hurt, Nick. I'm so glad you've come out of it." She moved closer and took his hand in hers. "How do you feel?"

Nick's health gradually improved, and he learned more about what had happened at the end of the battle. Apparently, the Thorn that attacked him was the one that he had seen leading the others, because when it was killed, the others withdrew in disorganized haste, passing water as they flew.

Then, for a long time, the defenders waited, fearing their return. But they didn't come back. Before long, the dead bodies surrounding the space module created such a stench that the ship had to be moved. Matt, with the help of Ruskin and Tara, dismantled what remained of the broken defense barrier and selected a site closer to the oil fields. The new location was on higher ground, not far from the old site, and was situated at the base of a small hill covered with mixed grassland and small trees. Matt, with some help from Tara, whom he taught to check the coordinates, had eased the module up and over to the new location.

Nick began to enjoy the days of his recuperation. While Matt spent much of his time away, exploring for more oil, Tara became a regular visitor. She came each day after work, and she often stayed to make supper for him and Matt. Frequently she would bring in meals she had prepared herself. Nick and Matt grew to appreciate the native food and began to look forward to it. Tara, in turn, learned some of their card games, and more than once, Ruskin joined them for dinner and cards to make a foursome.

Nick delighted in having Tara around. Her cheerful demeanor and ready sense of humor made the cabin feel lived in and more homelike. She talked about goings on in the town, about some of the children she taught, and about Ruskin's extensive laboratory and pharmacopoeia. She described the three doctors who worked there and explained how they prescribed curatives for all types of ailments and injuries. Twelve others worked in the lab, which besides the medicinal facilities, also had sections dedicated to agricultural and biological studies.

What interested Nick most was an upcoming trip that Ruskin had planned for the purpose of harvesting wild medicinal plants. Nick was interested, not just because he had taken courses in biology and botany in college. He had learned that Ruskin was also going to be on the lookout for herbs that might decrease his allergic reaction to Tara. When Nick told Tara that he might like to go with them, she was enthused. She told him they would be leaving during her break from teaching, and as part of an apprenticeship program, two students would also be going along.

Nick talked to Matt about it later that night. As he expected, Matt didn't like the idea. He had been on the planet long enough and wanted to finish the job so he could go home. Nick understood his point of view but reasoned that since Matt had been doing most of the work already, and there wasn't that much left to do, having two in the field wouldn't speed things up that much. Since they had only one car, they could only work one site at a time anyway. In the end, Matt stopped disagreeing. He knew, of course, that Nick was attracted to Tara, and he was good-natured enough that he could accord him some time off for "affairs of the heart" if necessary. He asked one question.

"Will you stay here with her if you do find a cure?"

"I don't know," Nick answered truthfully.

Later that night, as he lay in his bed, he thought again about Matt's question. What *did* he really want to do? The idea of leaving her forever was difficult to contemplate. Would he instead want to take her back with him, assuming she would be willing to go? Did he want to stay with her in Crystal? He mulled the possibilities for a long time, deciding finally that he just didn't know the answer. In time, he might know, but time was one thing he didn't have. He knew he couldn't keep Matt waiting much longer.

The next day he went with Tara to see the laboratory for himself. He was feeling much better by now and knew that walking would be good for him. After seeing the lab, he was impressed. Although they were unaccomplished in industrial processes and transportation, the community had made strides in biology and chemistry. Inside the "lab," as they called it, he was invited to look at different organic cultures through surprisingly powerful hand crafted microscopes. He saw diatomic algae being propagated for the relief of sore throat, and he met some of the technicians, learning a little about their current projects. Although much of the work was of a routine nature, such as preparing specific antidotes at designated potencies, research was also being conducted.

Nick enjoyed talking with the people there and was pleased that he was able to understand much of what they were saying. Tara showed him around the laboratory with obvious pride in her grandfather's life work. Nick could tell she was gratified that he didn't think it primitive. On the contrary, he assured her, it wasn't. He talked with Ruskin, who was, in an orderly and systematic way, making preparations for the trip. Ruskin discussed it briefly and, in answer to Nick's question, explained how his allergy to Tara might be suppressed.

When Nick asked if he could come along, Ruskin genuinely welcomed him, saying, "You can learn a lot on this trip, if you're interested in herbal medicine."

Over the next several days, Nick and Matt worked together in the oil fields taking samples and recording data to try to quantify the full extent of their find. It was dull, repetitious work, but it had to be done. Now that they had indeed found oil, they needed to complete all the necessary paperwork and fill in the numbers, so that the statisticians could make their feasibility determinations. Then, if they gave the go-ahead, a subsidiary of the Worlds' Bank would authorize a loan to cover the huge cost of sending ships and equipment to extract the oil and bring it back for refining. Nothing happened unless the managers in the big offices gave their OK, and unless the paperwork was completed *their* way, chances are nothing would happen.

Nick often thought of Tara as he worked. Wanting to help Matt get as much done as possible before leaving, he had not visited her since returning to the job, and he found it harder than he realized to be away from her. The day of the expedition finally arrived, and early that morning Matt dropped him off at the house.

It was a beautiful day. The sun was just rising, and there was a fragrant quality to the air. Many of the trees had a fresh growth of pale green leaves, and after last night's gentle rain, everything seemed to glisten in the light of the morning sun. Spring had arrived.

Tara looked up from attending to the forcs, saw Nick coming, and ran to meet him. Nick quickened his pace, and they embraced as they met. The tension he had felt over the past few days melted in her presence. As they walked together, hand in hand, she introduced him to the two young apprentices, Jon and Erik. Jon, who was fourteen, was the more slender and the taller of the two. Erik was twelve, comparatively husky, with reddish brown hair. Tara told Nick that they were two of her better trainees and that they were quite interested in learning more about medicine.

Ruskin came out of the house and wished them all a good morning as he sauntered down the steps, carrying an assortment of gear, which he handed to the boys. "Fine day," he said, and he looked around to check that everything was in order.

Altogether, they made up a fair-sized entourage. Seven forcs were at ready, one for each of the travelers and two more that were saddled with provisions and gear.

Ruskin gathered everyone together and said, "As you know, this is an important mission that we're beginning today." He looked toward the two youth. "We can enjoy each other's company and have some fun, but for you apprentices, these days should be mainly a learning experience. Tara has told me you both want to become practitioners. She has recommended you to me, and, as you know, not many have the chance you have to go on an expedition like this. The significance of our mission, however, is more important than that. People here are depending on us. Their health is at stake. That's why you must follow our directions precisely. As for the trip itself, it will be long and at times arduous. You have been told all this already." He glanced from the boys to Nick and Tara, and then, getting on his steed and raising his hand, he said, "Let's go."

They quickly mounted and were off, with Ruskin in the lead followed by Tara and Nick, Jon and Erik, and the two pack animals in the rear. As they traveled along, Tara frequently rode up to talk to Ruskin, and Nick often talked with the boys. Although the youths were not yet very good at thought transference, Nick had already learned enough language that he could understand and make himself understood by them most of the time. He was impressed that, despite their ages, they were quite intent and serious about the trip. This was especially true of Jon. Nick sensed that for him the journey was truly a personal mission, and that he was ready and willing to do anything that might be asked of him.

Erik, on the other hand, although committed, was fundamentally more fun loving and more easily distracted. As for Nick himself, he knew why he was going, or did he? Certainly, he liked being in Tara's company. Besides that, he decided he would learn what he could and enjoy the trip. As they emerged from some trees, she pointed out an escarpment rising to the left and said they would encounter territory that was more mountainous and eventually would have to dismount. The excursion was longer than it needed to be because they had decided to circle around the nesting area of the Thorns, even though they were assumed to be dangerous only during the month of Ravidian.

As the expedition continued through the day, the terrain became more scenic and wooded. Outcroppings of rock appeared on the hills, and when they reached the higher elevations they looked down on small lakes and streams that meandered across the countryside. The air, borne by southerly breezes, was warm and fresh and carried the scent of pines and other heady smells he could not identify.

Although they had not yet reached any mountains, it was apparent they were gradually gaining altitude, though at times they seemed to descend from their generally upward trek. With an hour still left before sunset, Ruskin signaled a halt. They were situated on one side of a meadowland, that sloped down to a valley of short, thick grass, ending in a small stream. Above, a sizeable cliff jutted out of the grass, and on top of the hill, short trees swayed in the breeze.

"Let's stop here," said Ruskin. "We'll have time to put up the tent and find some vegetables before the sun goes down. Jon, Erik, help me get the tent set up. Tara, would you and Nick find some greens and gather some firewood?"

As they dismounted, Tara beckoned Nick to follow her. They set off, going up the side of the hill toward the cliff near the top. When they reached it, they were both breathing heavily. She took his hand, and they looked out over the beautiful valley and surrounding plain beneath them. Then they turned to the sparse woods that began behind the rocks of the cliff.

Tara led the way, holding his hand, and before long she stopped to show him a broad leafed, serrated edged plant called "rashanks," which she said was crispy and delicious. Next, with some difficulty, she pulled from the ground a waist-high plant with deeply lobed bluish green leaves. Turning it over, she showed him how to remove the orangish outer covering from the rootstock. The creamy white inner root looked much like a carrot. "This is panga," she said, breaking off a piece and handing it to him. "I think you'll like it."

He took it from her and cautiously bit off the tip and chewed it. He smiled and took another bite. "It's very good. I hope we can find more of it."

"There's more over there," she answered, pointing toward the right, about fifty feet ahead. "You can help me get them out." They walked over to the bluish-green plants, and soon they had pulled a dozen nice-size stalks. They spent more time gathering food and then picked up some wood for the fire. With arms full, they returned to the campsite. The large tent was erected, and the boys were running, stopping, and then running again, playing a game with a ball they had brought with them. Ruskin was coming from the creek carrying a small pail of water, and he waved when he saw them approaching.

Soon they had the fire going, and the smoked venison was boiling in a pot as darkness settled around them. By this time they were all hungry, and they chatted as they lined up for the delicious smelling hot venison and steamed vegetables that Tara was serving. Nick sat down and waited for her to join him. Ruskin gave thanks for the food, and they ate heartily as the last traces of light left the sky. The utter darkness was relieved only by the flickering of the campfire and the points of light glowing in the night sky .

Relaxing by the embers, they discussed the trip in general, what tomorrow would bring, and the kinds of plants they would be looking for. After awhile, the boys went into the tent to go to bed. Ruskin grew silent, puffing contentedly on a lit stem, while staring into the fire. Who knew what thoughts were going through his head? Soon he too said goodnight and disappeared into the tent. Tara was sitting next to Nick, and she leaned toward him. He put his arms around her, and they watched together the glow from the fire and the resplendent twinkling of the stars that filled the sky above them. "Can you tell which sun is yours," she asked, as she languidly lay back in his arms.

"Yes. It's the small star over there, down from the bright bluish one."

"That little one there?" she asked, pointing to it.

"Yes, that's the one."

"Does our sun look that small too?"

"Oh, yes. Just as small as ours at this distance."

"Amazing," she concluded, as she nestled in his arms. Then she sat up straight. "We better get some sleep. As soon as daylight breaks, grandpa will want to get going."

They entered the tent together and in the darkness could barely make out the sleeping arrangements. As their eyes adapted, they could tell that the boys were on one side of the tent and Ruskin was in the middle, lightly snoring. Nick and Tara's bedding was already laid out on the other side.

Nick went to the edge of the tent, removed his shoes and outer clothes, and tucked himself in. Tara waited briefly before coming to bed. Nick was tired, and his sleeping bag was surprisingly comfortable, so he didn't think he would have any trouble falling asleep. Nevertheless, he did, and as time passed, he found himself staring wide-awake at the top of the tent. Hearing Tara turn in her bed, he whispered, "are you still awake?"

"Yes, I can't sleep," she answered.

He rolled over and found himself at her side. Placing his arm around her, he felt the narrowness of her waist. He experienced a rush of tenderness toward her and whispered, "I wish I could kiss you."

"Me too," she answered, stretching her arms out to hold him.

"I've wanted to hold you like this ever since I left you that first night at your house," he said.

"I've been dreaming of you holding me," she whispered, her body trembling slightly.

"Are you cold?"

"No," she said, smiling, her body relaxing more in his arms. "I've never been held by anyone like this before. It makes me feel so good to be in your arms."

"Yes," he replied, as he pondered the mystery of a girl so beautiful who had experienced so little. He touched her face and bent down to kiss her underneath her chin, near the nape of her neck. He felt her soft breathing and the rise and fall of her breast. She held him closer and closed her eyes. Then, suddenly letting go of him, she whispered, "Let's go outside."

"Why?"

"Just come," she said softly.

Nick felt around for his clothes and shoes, put them on, and finding his way to the tent entrance, met Tara there and took her hand.

"Let's go up there on the knoll," she said, pointing toward the hill that was barely visible in the darkness. The night was still warm, and a quiet breeze moved the air around them. They reached the top of the knoll and sat down together. The valley was spread out beneath them, and the stars shimmered above. "Have you made any plans for the future?" she asked.

He put his arm around her waist, and answered, "Yes, I've thought a lot about the future. I was planning to make a lot of money, settle down, raise a family, and travel with them all over the universe. Lately I've been rethinking some of my plans. I don't think that making a lot of money is so important anymore."

"I understand that you need it to travel," she interjected. "Wouldn't you miss that?"

"No, I don't think so. Not anymore. You see," he continued, looking into her eyes, "I had a girl when I left Earth several months ago. Now I can scarcely remember her features. Someone else has replaced her image in my mind. I think you know who that is." He embraced her, and she spontaneously returned his embrace, but then abruptly turned away again.

"When you get to the next planet will you forget about me too?"

"I don't think so," he said, noncommittally. "How could I ever forget you? Besides, maybe I won't leave."

"Really?" she exclaimed, thrilled by the revelation. "Wouldn't you miss everyone back at your home town?"

"Tara, if we can cure my allergy problem, would you marry me?" he asked.

She tilted her head to face him directly, and in the starlight he could see tears glistening in her eyes. "That would make me so happy, Nick, if I could really be your bride. The thing is, here we marry until death, and that is the only way I would want to marry you. I understand that on your world people often wed for a time. Nick, I couldn't do that. It would break my heart."

Nick saw tears run down her cheeks. "I know, it's true; many on Earth do that. "Tara," he said emphatically, "I would never want to leave you. By my God and yours, I swear that I would never leave you. I want to love you till we're both old and gray."

"Then I will love you that long, too," she replied, taking his hands in hers and holding them tightly in her lap.

Nick leaned over to kiss her.

"No. You can't!" she said quickly.

"Damn! I forgot." He took her hand; they got up and walked together down the hill back to the tent.

Chapter Six

When Nick wakened the next morning, it wasn't just the dawning of a new day. He was elated and found it difficult to calmly eat breakfast, chatting casually, when he felt like making an announcement to the universe about the two of them. Furthermore, what he really wanted to do was to take her away with him, to a place where he could hold her and love her. If only he could be sure that there was a cure for his allergy. There must be one! At the moment Ruskin's relaxed and ordinarily stimulating conversation held little interest for him, as there was so much he wanted to talk about with Tara. Still, everything hinged on the problem. He told himself to calm down and be patient. There was nothing that could be done about it now. They would have to wait until the expedition was finished before any cure could be attempted. In the meantime he would have to live one day at a time while hoping for the best.

He listened as Ruskin talked about the territory they would reach today and the types of plants and minerals they would be looking for. Nick had come to admire his low-key, knowledgeable style. Quietly enthusiastic about his subject, he was always ready to answer questions and to explain the uses of the herbs and succulents that they were collecting.

They finished breakfast, packed up their equipment, and started leaving the campsite. Just then an unlikely looking trio appeared from the other side of the nearby hill. Three large men, dressed in dark brown robes, ambled toward them. They had an expectant look on their faces. Nick glanced at Tara, who smiled and said, "They're mendicants."

Ruskin stopped, and they watched as the three lined up in front of them, bowed deeply, and in unison rubbed their hands together. Then the one in the middle, who was also the largest, raised his head and intoned in a deep, soulful voice; "We are the Brothers of Midian, who have unfortunately fallen on hard times. Although you can see the coarseness of our garb and the sorrowfulness of our demeanor, we are too proud to beg."

"Sirs, if you have need of food, we will give you some. However, we don't have a lot to share as we still have a long way to go," said Ruskin.

"Oh no, kind sir," spoke the one on the right, the smallest. "Although verily, we are hungry, we cannot take from your stores without giving you some measure of recompense." So saying, he picked up the provisions that Ruskin had already unpacked for them.

"All right," Ruskin replied, dismounting, though obviously impatient to get underway. "We will stop for a short time if you insist."

The rest of them also dismounted and sat down at the base of the small hill to their right. The three men huddled together, heads bent down, as if deciding what they were going to do. Suddenly, they separated and started yelling at the top of their lungs, running and zigzagging in every direction. Abruptly, they stopped. The boys thought their short spectacle was hilarious, and they shouted, "More! More!"

The three looked up and acknowledged their audience with a bow. Then they sprang into action again, turning cartwheels, jumping over each other's backs, doing flips and pirouettes, all while yelling like madmen. Their agility was amazing, especially for such heavy men. Judging by the perspiration on their faces, they definitely put everything into their performance.

Ludicrous as their presentation was, Nick began to feel admiration for them. They weren't done yet. Looking around for a podium, they found a large rock and rolled it into place. The largest mendicant climbed on top while the other two stood on each side facing their audience. He addressed them:

> "We are the men of Mendax,
> the strangers in your midst.
> We come from many miles away,
> To please you is our wish.
>
> And if our crazy antics,
> Make your spirits glow,
> Our mission is accomplished,
> and we are free to go.
>
> We thank you for your patronage,
> and thank you for your bread,
> and now we must be moving on,
> glad to be well fed."

After saying this, he jumped down from the rock, and the three of them marched in single file to the east, humming a tune. Stunned, their audience continued to sit there watching them go until Nick broke the silence. "What a show!"

"They must have done it for the boys. I've never seen them go on like that," enthused Tara.

"Then you know them?" Nick asked.

"We've seen them before, but we don't really know them," answered Ruskin. "I think they come from a small settlement a long way from here."

"I've seen them twice before, but this is the first time they did acrobatics," added Tara.

"Yes, any time they've been around in the past, they've recited poetry or given little speeches. Looks like they've broadened their act," said Ruskin.

"It was so unexpected to see such heavy men tumbling," Nick remarked. "For me, that's what made it so funny."

"I don't think any of us will forget that act," reflected Tara.

Ruskin mounted his forc, and, following his lead, the small group started out again. As they traveled on, the sun rose high above them, and the terrain became rough and mountainous. They were definitely gaining altitude. The sky was a bright blue with white clouds that drifted by. The air grew cooler and breezier, the trees were sparser, and rocks appeared more frequently. Whenever they had steep hills to climb, they dismounted and led the animals along the trail, a precaution they took to keep them from slipping and possibly breaking a leg. It was slow going, and when they stopped for an afternoon lunch break, they were glad to rest.

Nick was amazed at Ruskin's endurance. He appeared to be no more breathless than anyone else. While the adults took their time eating, Jon and Erik finished quickly and scampered up a steep hill. Soon they had disappeared. When they were ready to leave, Tara called out to them, but the boys didn't answer. Nick started up the hill to look for them, and Tara joined him. As they neared the top, they saw a terrible sight in the sky above them. Flying, about one hundred feet overhead, was a large Thorn.

Nick and Tara exchanged anxious glances and hurried the rest of the way up. From their high vantage point, they anxiously scanned the area, trying to spot the boys. They were nowhere to be seen. Not knowing how the Thorns would react in their own territory, they were reluctant to draw attention to themselves by calling out, and yet they were becoming increasingly worried about Jon and Erik.

"If you go down that way, I'll check this way," said Nick, pointing out directions. "But let's not get too far apart."

He started descending the right side of the hill and saw Tara a moment before she disappeared through the trees on his left. Rather suddenly it became much darker, as a cloud covered the sun, and Nick entered a dense, forested area. Surprisingly, the wind seemed to be blowing stronger and cooler through the valley, and he began to wonder if his imagination was playing tricks on him. He surveyed the area around him through the tree trunks and still saw no sign of the boys or of anything else out of the ordinary. Then he heard Tara's faint cry in the distance. He answered her call, not knowing if she heard him, and advanced quickly in the direction of her voice. Soon, he saw her through the bushes. She was with Jon and Erik. "Are you all right?" he asked.

"We're fine," she replied. "Jon and Erik have something to show you."

"Look at that!" said Erik with excitement, as he lifted his jacket off a large, white object. To Nick's astonishment, there, lying on the ground, was a huge egg. It must have been almost a foot and a half long and a foot thick.

"Oh, no. Is that what I think it is?" he asked, looking at Tara.

"I think so," she replied. "I'm surprised it hasn't hatched by now."

"Where did you find this?" he asked, speaking to Jon and Erik.

"Over there," they answered in unison, and Erik pointed to a hill about two hundred feet away from them.

"It was near the bottom of that hill," added Jon. "Maybe it rolled down from the top."

"We better leave," declared Tara, apprehensively glancing upwards. "Look!" she said, pointing to the sky where a Thorn circled lazily overhead.

"Into the woods!" Nick whispered. They all rushed toward the protection of the trees. From beneath the branches, they tried to follow the Thorns movements. Soon, it was out of sight, and they could breathe easier.

After climbing back up the hill, they went down the other side to where they had left Ruskin. They anticipated that he would be worried about them. Instead, they found him sleeping peacefully in the sunlight.

"Grandpa," said Tara softly, putting her hand on his shoulder. He woke with a start, slowly looked around him and then up at Tara. He seemed slightly chagrined to have been found sleeping, and Tara smiled at him saying, "We're ready to go now, grandpa."

As they continued along their route, they filled him in on their adventure. He was concerned, and wanted to know everything about it. He concluded, however, that he didn't think the Thorns would be much of a threat during any other month than Ravidian.

The trail was rougher now. They climbed over hills and down valleys and forded small streams. Now, more often than not, they had to dismount and lead their forcs behind them. The scenery was spectacular; but their muscles were sore, and their breathing was heavy. Finally Ruskin stopped and said, "Let's camp here tonight." It was earlier in the evening than usual.

After supper they felt reinvigorated. There was a small lake nearby, and Jon and Erik were anxious to go swimming. Nick wanted to bathe, and together he and the boys walked over to the lake. The water was cool though not cold, and soon they had undressed and were all splashing in the nude. The boys found a small ridge overlooking the lake, climbed it, and jumped in. Enjoying the leap immensely, they returned again and again to the cliff, and Nick began tossing their ball toward them as they jumped. It was great fun for them to try to catch it out of the air as they fell. They were having such a good time, Nick tried it also. As he came up from his dive, he caught sight of Ruskin bathing about two hundred yards away. Then he heard Tara call out, "When are you boys going to be finished?"

"Where are you?" he asked, still not able to see her.

"Over here," she answered. "I'd like to bathe, too, when you're done."

"Come join us," he invited.

"No. No thank you," she replied. "I'm not coming in till you're gone."

"Boys, I think we've had enough swimming for today," said Nick.

"Aw," complained Erik. "I want to play some more. Just a little longer, please?"

"Let them play awhile longer," said Tara. "I'll wait." She still was not visible to Nick through the bushes.

"Where are you?" he asked again, trying to get a glimpse of her.

"I'll tell you when you're dressed," she answered.

Nick climbed out of the water, dried off, and began putting his clothes on. Before he had his shirt on, he heard branches rustling, and Tara stepped out of the bushes. She openly admired his muscular upper body.

"Did you really expect me to come in with you?" she asked.

"It would have been nice," he nonchalantly answered, as he pulled on his shirt.

"Jon. Erik." he called out. "Let's get out now."

"Thanks," she said, stepping forward to give him a quick hug.

The next day they slept a little later, and after a quick breakfast, soon were hiking swiftly toward the sea. They all were enthusiastic because today, if they pressed on, they would finally reach their destination. Tara had been there once, many years before. Only Ruskin was perfectly sure of the way, and he led on relentlessly.

"Hey! Wait for me," Erik cried out from behind the pack animals.

"Yes, Grandpa, don't you think we should take a rest?" asked Tara.

"Of course we can," Ruskin replied. "I guess I get a little excited when we get this close. Yes, let's stop for lunch. I'm ready to eat. How about the rest of you?"

They ate together in the lower level of a mountain whose summit they had climbed earlier, and the cool sea breezes rippled through their hair. They didn't want to lose too much time, and soon they were on the way again. By early afternoon they had reached the crest of a hill where they could see the inlet of the sea. "There it is, down there," Ruskin pointed out triumphantly.

The rest of them shaded their eyes from the sun and looked out. "Oh, I see it." yelled Tara, as she stood on her tiptoes. "See it, over there." she pointed it out to Nick.

"OK., I see it now," he said. "It's still a long way off."

"Well, it's a downhill trip from here," said Ruskin. "We'll be there before nightfall."

It turned out to be a very long trek down to the lagoon, and as the five weary travelers set up the tent and prepared a late evening meal, they knew everything would have to wait until tomorrow.

That night, after they had eaten, and the others had gone to bed, Nick and Tara spread a blanket on the ground and sat looking out over the landscape and up at the stars. Tara snuggled next to Nick to keep warm. "Tell me about the stars, Nick. It's a very different world out there, isn't it?"

"Many different worlds. Some, like the one I come from, are densely populated and very automated. Others, like that blue star there," he pointed to it, "has a habitable planet, but few people live there because the weather is hot all the time. Many of the stars have celestial bodies circling them, but few of those have habitable conditions where people could live without building major life support systems. Still, there are more than enough livable places out there to satisfy population needs. The problem in recent decades has been a lack of enough energy resources to support the growing number of inhabitants. See that large red star up there?" He pointed it out.

"The one that forms a triangle with the bright yellow stars?"

"Yes, that's the one. Its name is Antares, and it's where the oil freighters have been most active. It has a smaller star in a distant orbit around it and several planets, two of which have supplied almost thirty percent of the oil needs used by the eastern half of the galaxy for the past fifty years."

"That sounds like a lot."

"It definitely is," he agreed. "Unfortunately, the oil fields there are gradually being depleted, and with scarcity there's more of a chance that a war might be fought over the limited supply.

"Are there many worlds that are being supplied with oil?"

"Oh, yes. Thirty-seven to be exact, although some of those have only minimal need"

"If you could go anywhere, to any of the worlds, where would you go?"

"Well, I haven't been to all that many, but for a vacation Olanda looks the nicest on EV. It's a tropical paradise with floating islands drifting in a warm sea. There are all kinds of fruit trees ready to be plucked, and I understand the natives are very hospitable."

"That sounds beautiful. You mean the islands are actually drifting in the sea?"

"Yes, from what I've heard, they are only a few feet thick in most places, and they actually float."

"Amazing. I'd like to go there too."

"I'd love to take you there, but it might not be possible unless they come to extract the oil we found here. I'm not so sure I would want that anymore. It might bring too many changes to your beautiful planet."

"Our beautiful planet," she corrected him, as she leaned toward him.

"Yes. *Our* beautiful planet," he repeated, as he held her close.

When the sun rose the next morning, Nick was the first to stir. He quietly slipped on his shoes and jacket, and stepped out of the tent. He walked to the edge of the lagoon to see what it looked like in daylight. To his surprise, it was dry. Instead of water, the surface was covered with sparse grass that erupted in various places with short, strange looking plants of many shades and colors.

He cautiously stepped down onto the flat, brownish surface. It supported him, and he could feel the buoyancy of the water underneath. He took a few steps and felt the surface sway beneath his feet. It was one of the strangest sensations he had ever experienced. He was afraid to go out much further before finding out if it was safe. He carefully walked back to the edge and was glad to be back on solid ground again.

Back at the campsite, Tara was preparing breakfast, and Ruskin was busily at work preparing vials and adding labels to most of them.

"Where'd you go?" she asked, looking up from her cooking.

"Just over to the lagoon," he answered as he came up and stood behind her. "Smells delicious," he said, nuzzling her with his chin.

"What, me or the food?" she replied, her hands occupied with cooking.

"Both. Say, did you know the lagoon is covered with plants? I mean, you can't even see the water."

"Of course. It's always that way," she replied, surprised that he would mention it.

"I've never experienced anything like it. Is it safe to walk on?"

"It's fairly safe, but you have to be careful, especially where the plants come up. In places where there is a lot of vegetation, they weaken the surface of the mat. Also, you have to be careful not to walk too far toward the center of the lagoon because there the mat thins out until it's all open water."

"Unusual. What is it made of?"

"It's just matted vegetation and humus that floats up on top. "You mean you don't have anything like it on Earth?"

"Not that I'm aware of. At least not so thick that it can be walked on. The whole basin must be full of nutrients to support vegetation that thick."

"I never really thought much about it," she replied. "There is a stream that feeds the lagoon and empties into the sea through the coral reef. Ruskin says that it's the mix of fresh water and seawater that produces the great variety of plants in the pond. On this side there are mostly freshwater plants, but toward the reef there are plants that have adapted to seawater."

"I can see why this is such a botanical gold mine."

"Gold? What is that?"

"I'll tell you about it at breakfast. Will it be ready soon?"

As they ate, Nick told Tara about the precious metal, and then Ruskin briefed them on what they would be collecting. He urged them to be careful, pointing out the dangers, and took special pains to talk to

Erik and Jon about safety. As always, he instructed them on what to look for and whether to harvest the roots, stem, leaves, blossoms, or fruit of the plant. He emphasized that they should be on the lookout for certain rare plants and for others that were especially beneficial.

Then, as an extra precaution, he told Jon and Erik to stay together at all times while on the lagoon's surface. With that, they loaded up their specimen bags, vials, and drying nets.

Dividing the area into sections, Ruskin assigned one to the boys, adjacent ones to Nick and Tara, and an area for himself. As Nick and Tara walked together to their areas, she showed him that there was little to fear from walking on the floating vegetation, and as they continued over its surface, he lost his sense of unsteadiness and instead marveled at the softness with which the underlying water cushioned his step.

By the time they separated, he was eager to begin collecting. He was impressed at the variety of vegetation to be found in one place. Soon, he was absorbed in wandering from one plant to the next, selecting nice specimens, pruning, marking, and dropping them in his bags. He glanced at Tara from time to time, to see that he didn't get too far away from her, and could see that she was also engrossed in the work. It was a calm, peaceful day under a mostly sunny sky, and he was content to spend the whole day there.

Then, a loud shout broke through the early afternoon stillness. It was Jon, and he frantically called out to them. All three of them started running toward him, though from their distance he appeared as just a small figure on the horizon. After running swiftly for over a minute, Nick arrived to find Jon crying, hysterically pointing at a large hole in the floating mat. "Erik's under there!" he shouted.

By the time Tara and Ruskin arrived breathless on the scene, Nick was poised to jump in after Erik.

"Wait!" shouted Ruskin. "Here, hold on to this rope so you'll be able to find your way back to the opening." Nick grabbed the rope, took a deep breath, and dove in. The water was so black, he couldn't see a thing. He circled around near the top, frequently bumping his head on the bushy bottom of the mat surface. He was beginning to run out of air when he nudged something soft and solid. It was Erik. Grabbing his arm, he jerked on the rope with his free hand and felt himself being drawn rapidly toward the hole in the mat. He pushed Erik's lifeless body up onto the surface and gasped for air. With his knees pressed against the sod, he took Ruskin's hand and climbed out of the water.

Quickly, he turned Erik over, and taking one look at his blue, lifeless body, he knelt down and started mouth-to-mouth resuscitation. For what seemed like a long time, nothing happened. Then Erik drew his legs up and simultaneously coughed and threw up. He opened his eyes and looked at them vacantly. Nick helped him to sit up and thumped him solidly on the back. Erik coughed up some more water and began breathing normally.

Tara, seeing that he was all right, sat down beside him and caressed him. "Oh, Erik, we're so glad you're OK. We were so worried about you. How do you feel?"

"I feel sick," he answered.

Ruskin approached Nick and in a low, awed voice said, "Nick, that boy was dead. What kind of power do you have? You breathed life into a dead body."

Nick took a step back. "Ruskin, it's not supernatural. It's mouth-to-mouth resuscitation, something we practice in training back on Earth. Erik wasn't dead, only unconscious from lack of air. What I did was get air back into his lungs. When it's done in time, anyone, just like Erik, may regain consciousness and start breathing on their own again."

"Well, that's simply amazing. We should definitely learn how to do that," he said to Tara. "In fact, everyone in the lab should be taught it. Nick, this is too good not to pass on. Will you teach us the technique and all the parameters for using it when we get back?"

"Yes, of course. This method is much better than the one that they used to use on Earth centuries ago. It will work even if a lung is partially collapsed. Once I'm cured of my allergy to your granddaughter, she and I can demonstrate it at the Lab." Turning to Tara, who was still comforting Erik, he spoke a little louder, "Tara, you'll help me demonstrate mouth-to-mouth resuscitation won't you?" She looked up from Erik and smiled, without saying a word.

For the next two days they gathered specimens, then brought them back to the camp to be catalogued and packaged. Ruskin stayed up late at night tallying the results of the day's collection. He was very pleased with the quality and quantity of their procurements and congratulated them heartily. "You have all done a terrific job," he told them on the eve of their departure. "We can stock our laboratory for at least two years with all the specimens you have obtained. Jon, Erik,

I congratulate you and welcome you to the lab when you finish your studies."

Chapter Seven

Over the next several days, they proceeded to make the long trip home. Nick and Tara continued to meet late in the evening after the others had settled in. They looked forward to these times when they could be alone and talk. They discussed many things, the customs of Earth, versus those of Crystal, and their own ideas about life and love. They agreed that they would marry if the allergic condition could be overcome. The "if" was troubling them, however, and just as troubling to Tara was her suspicion that the treatment itself would be dangerous for Nick.

Love Strokes
223

At last, they arrived back in Crystal and went directly to the Laboratory. There everyone enthusiastically welcomed the tired travelers. Entering the main lab room, they were glad to remove their heavy packs and sit down to drink big glasses of fresh guava. The staff was happy to see them back, and they crowded around them. Most were also very interested in seeing all that they had collected. Ruskin sat down on a stool and talked about the trip and about the various rare plants they had found. He spoke in general terms, promising he would make a complete report later.

One man, whose name was Range, asked if they had seen any Thorns. Ruskin motioned to Nick, who got up from his chair to tell them about the incident with the Thorn and the egg. Range questioned him further and was quite interested in anything Nick could tell him about the Thorns. The two of them agreed to meet at another time to talk more about them.

More time passed, and Nick was ready to leave, but he could see that Tara was engrossed in conversation with a sandy-haired, intelligent looking man, so he waited for her. A young, pretty girl remained with him after the others had left. She regarded him candidly and asked if he was tired after the long trip. Nick admitted he was and with a look of concern she offered to get him more to drink. She told him she wished that she also could have gone on the trip. Nick learned that her name was Trila and that though she was only seventeen, she was already a receptionist and lab assistant. She said that she knew something about him already from her cousin, Tara. Nick got the impression that the dark-haired girl had somehow acquired a very high opinion of him, and he looked around somewhat uncomfortably to see if Tara was finished talking. As she caught his eye, he excused himself from Trila and went over to her.

"Can you come with me back to the house now?" she asked.

"Yes," he answered, unable to tell what she had in mind.

Upon leaving the lab, and walking with Tara in the cool night air, he quickly felt refreshed. "Who was that man you were talking with so intently," he asked, trying to make sure he didn't betray the tinge of jealously he felt.

"Why, that's Dr. Gefert," she replied. "He's our best allergy specialist. In fact, he's the one who will be your doctor."

"I'd like to begin the treatment as soon as possible."

"I'm afraid it's not going to be easy for you. Are you sure you want to do this?"

"Yes, whatever it takes," he answered quickly. "I can't say I'm good with pain, but being without you would be worse."

"I'm worried, Nick. Dr. Gefert believes that what he proposes to do will work, but even he's not certain. What scares me is that there is a chance the treatment could seriously hurt you. I mean what if the medicine triggers some kind of unexpected reaction in your body that our doctors aren't prepared for? What if. . ."

"Tara, please stop worrying. You're scaring me too. We've talked about this many times, and we know there is some risk. The risk is worth it to me. Isn't it worth it to you?"

"Yes, yes! It is, Nick. I'm sorry. You know it's what I want, too. I just don't know what I would do if . . ." She wiped the tears from her eyes.

"Don't worry, darling. Everything will be all right. I'm strong and healthy, and with God's help, we're going to start a new generation, just the two of us. The best of both worlds."

Tara looked up at him and smiled through her tears. "Yes, my Earthman, you're right. We're going to do it together. We're going to be a family. We're going to conquer this thing and nothing's going to keep us apart." She stopped and appeared to think for a moment. Then, she spoke in a slower pace. "Before there's any children, there has to be a lot of love. That's very important." She looked back at him.

"Don't you know yet how much I love you?" he asked as he drew her closer to him.

"Yes," she replied simply, smiling as she nestled in his embrace.

Nick slept overnight on a cot at Tara's house, and early the next morning he left to go back to the ship. He arrived to find Matt eating breakfast. They were glad to see each other again. Nick ordered some breakfast for himself from the restant, and sitting down together, they talked at length about all that happened since they had last seen each other.

Nick told Matt about his growing relationship with Tara and his plans for a future with her, if he could overcome his reaction. He told him about the trip for medicinal plants and of saving Erik's life when he almost drowned.

Matt told Nick about the progress he had made in oil exploration and how, despite all his work, he still didn't know if the corporate office would consider the site large enough for commercial drilling. He showed Nick the trove of samples he had collected to take back for analysis and the wealth of data accumulated.

Nick was impressed. Matt had indeed worked assiduously in his absence. The delicate part Nick saved for last. He told Matt that he definitely planned to marry Tara, *if* the treatment, scheduled to start the next day, was successful. When Matt learned that there was some danger that Nick could be hurt by the therapy, he was concerned. In the end, since he couldn't get Nick to reconsider, he agreed to stay on for up to a week and a half. By that time they would know whether there would be a wedding or if Nick would need treatment, perhaps at a hospital on Earth.

Early the next morning Nick arrived as scheduled at the Laboratory. Dr. Gefert was attentive in his usual officious manner, and Tara was sweet and meek as a lamb, as she listened intently to everything the doctor said. In its details, it was a complex procedure that he described to them; but, in general, the plan called for a steady progression in the dosage of the allergen until immunity was obtained. Once that was achieved, boosters would be administered every two years as a protective measure.

The doctor explained rather mechanically how an extreme dilution of Tara's saliva, in a specifically selected herbal solution, would be used as the initial dose. He handed Nick the vial. Nick took it carefully in his hand, looked into Tara's eyes, and then quickly emptied the contents into his mouth and swallowed.

"I feel fine," he said as he leaned back on the bed. He didn't feel that way long. In a moment his head began swimming and his vision began losing clarity.

"Nick! Are you all right?" entreated Tara as she bent over his supine body, sensing that something was wrong.

"I feel dizzy. My head feels like it's spinning," he said with difficulty.

"We were expecting some disorientation and other physical manifestations at the outset," said Dr. Gefert.

Nick moaned as increasing pain rushed through his body.

"Doctor! Can't you do something?" cried Tara.

"No need to," he answered, completely unperturbed. He put his hands on Nick's head and neck and concentrated on what he felt there. Then he spoke again to Tara. "I expected this. When he comes out of it he will be on the way to overcoming the initial dosage."

"But surely it's not going to be necessary to knock him out with each dose!" she said heatedly.

"Do you want him cured?" he asked.

Tara nodded yes and tried to keep herself under control.

"Then we'll do it my way," he continued. "There is no easy way; you should know that. If we take things one step at a time, I'm confident he's going to make it. Cheer up, girl. He's a strong young man."

Tara took some heart in what Dr. Gefert said. She caressed Nick's limp body and waited, praying silently. She waited at his side for what seemed like a long time. Finally, she felt Nick's arm move. Then he shuddered and opened his eyes.

"Tara?" he whispered, in the darkened room.

"Yes, it's me," she responded eagerly. "How do you feel?"

"Terrible. I have a splitting headache, and I feel so cold."

"Here," she said, folding a thick blanket around him. "You've been unconscious for hours. Dr. Gefert predicted as much. He wants me to tell him when you wake up."

"I had such a strange dream," he continued, shaking off his grogginess. "A space cruiser was either coming or leaving, I don't know which. Anyway, as it reached the dark side of the planet, it exploded in a blinding flash of light. The fragments of the space vessel rained down on Bridestar, making brilliant arcs in the night sky. Then, and this is the odd part, the children of Crystal came out to gather up the chunks of melted fragments. They put them together in a pile and danced around them."

"That's eerie," she whispered. Getting up from the bed, she lit two wall sconces and said, "I better let Dr. Gefert know that you're awake." As she walked out, Nick tried to fathom what his strange dream might mean.

Soon the doctor returned with Tara at his side. "How do you feel?" he asked pleasantly.

"Not so good," Nick answered, turning his head from side to side. "My head feels like it was hit by a log."

"I'm not surprised. No nausea? That's good. Maybe I can do something for your headache. Here, bend over toward me." His skilled hands tapped on Nick's forehead then moved back, applying steady pressure back and forth along the top and sides of his cranium. "There," he said as he finished. "Does that feel any better?"

"A lot better."

"Now, don't get overanxious or exert yourself in any way," he cautioned. "You're going to need rest to get ready for the next concentration." Turning to Tara he said, "Please make sure he gets plenty of sleep and remains calm. If he's ready, we can continue tomorrow."

Nick didn't remember anything about the rest of the night. When he awoke, he could see through the gaps in the blinds that it was already bright outside. Tara was gone, and so was Dr. Gefert.

A girl entered carrying a tray. She opened the window slats, and sunlight splashed into the room. It was Trila, the young Lab assistant.

"Good morning," she said brightly. "I hope you're ready for breakfast."

"Definitely," he answered, returning her smile. "It seems like two days since I've eaten."

"If you sit up, I'll put a pillow behind your back, and then rest this on your lap, Mr. Bartok."

"Mr. Bartok. Where did you get the mister from? I haven't heard mister in front of my name since I left Earth."

"Well," she said, hesitating. "My cousin told me that on Earth people are addressed as Mr. or Mrs. or Ms. I hope I didn't use it in the wrong way."

"Not that you misapplied it, Trila, it just seems so foreign to me here. On Earth, mister is used for correspondence or when people don't know each other well. I'd like it if you just called me Nick."

"Oh, sure, I'd be happy too," she answered, glad to do without formalities.

"Tell me, what else has Tara been telling you about me?"

"Lots. How you piloted a huge ship between the stars. How you gave up wealth and family on Earth to find oil to warm the houses. How you fought valiantly to defeat the Thorns, and . . ."

"Wait a minute," he protested. "It seems you've been getting a rather idealistic picture of me."

"Well it's only the truth," said Tara, entering the room. "Trila and I are cousins and we also sometimes work together in the Lab. I couldn't keep quiet about you."

"I just hope you haven't deluded her into thinking that I'm some kind of hero," Nick replied.

Dr. Gefert strode into the room and, in his businesslike manner, said hello to Tara and Trila. "How do you feel today, Nick?"

"Much better, doctor. The headache is completely gone, and I feel fit and well rested."

"In that case we might as well go on to the next step. Why don't you take a few minutes and get some fresh air first. It's a fine day."

"That sounds like a good idea," Nick replied, glad for a chance to get out.

Nick and Tara walked together through the door and into the bright sunlight. They hadn't been outside long when Range hailed them.

"How's it going with the treatments, Nick?" he asked as he came up to them.

"So far, I've only had one, and it's definitely not been fun," he answered. "Tara is already planning for our wedding however, which you could take as a good sign that I'll pull through."

"Sure he will," she asserted spiritedly, leaning against Nick. "It's just a matter of time."

"Glad to hear that Nick. I've been thinking a lot about those Thorns. They've been getting more aggressive in recent years, and after the attack you fought off last Ravidian, I'm afraid of what might happen next year."

"You think they might be even more ferocious?" asked Tara.

"Yes I do, and, frankly, I don't like the idea of just waiting for them to come back. I think we should go after them on their own grounds and exterminate them."

Tara gasped. "That would be suicide!"

"Not if we have a plan and some pulsars. What do you think, Nick?"

"I like the idea," Nick reflected. "But it could backfire. I don't think that in the past the birds have thought that man was their natural enemy. Unfortunately, that could be changing. My concern is that if an attack failed, they might retaliate by attacking the town."

"My worry is that they might do that regardless," said Range.

"You may be right. In any event, we should make some plans. Want to work on it together?"

"Definitely," he answered, slapping him on the back so hard that Nick almost stumbled. "Count on me."

"Nick, we better go back to the clinic," broke in Tara. As soon as they were far enough away from Range, she stopped and faced him. "You're not really thinking of fighting the Thorns again?" she asked heatedly.

"Not immediately," he answered, squeezing her hand. "I think we need to be prepared though. Don't worry. I really don't want to take any unnecessary chances."

"I think you should just leave them alone," she said emphatically, shaking her head.

"Take it easy," he said, putting an arm around her shoulders. "If they leave us alone, we'll leave them alone. O.K.?"

"Do you promise?" she asked, concerned.

"I promise," he answered, giving her a hug. "We better go back. Dr. Gefert is probably waiting."

Nick reacted similarly to the next treatment as he had to the first. He blacked out, regaining consciousness with a splitting headache. In the days that followed, however, the dosage was gradually increased, while his reaction to it gradually decreased. Yet, whenever Nick or Tara asked Dr. Gefert about his progress, he seemed reluctant to talk about it. At last, in frustration, Tara asked him directly. "When will he be done with all this, doctor?"

"At this point, the only way you can be certain that our allergy desensitization program has achieved its objective is to test it in a natural setting without any laboratory controls."

"Do you mean we're done?" asked Tara.

"I think so. I'm going to give you these three vials just in case. Take one immediately with water if you notice any discomfort following contact. Let me know how it goes."

"We will be glad to try it out, doctor," said Nick, smiling as he placed his left arm around Tara. Extending his free hand, he added, "We want to thank you so much for everything you've done and want to invite you to the wedding."

"I shall be happy to join you." They shook hands.

Nick and Tara strolled out of the clinic, and turned to kiss on the doorstep.

"I don't feel a thing," said Nick, after their long kiss.

"I do," she said, looking at him attentively. "Are you sure you don't feel anything?"

"Yes. Really, I don't feel anything at all."

Love Strokes

She turned to kiss him again, a long, ardent kiss. Some passersby turned to stare at them. As they parted, she gazed dreamily into his eyes. "Do you feel anything now?" she whispered.

"Yes," he responded huskily, pulling her tighter to him. "I definitely feel it."

"Nick!" A loud voice pierced their absorption with each other.

"Matt," they echoed as he quickly joined them.

"I want to congratulate you and Tara before I leave. I heard you've made good progress in overcoming the allergy."

"Thank you. We sure owe a lot to Dr. Gefert and the lab team. You don't have to leave right away, do you Matt?

"Yes, unfortunately. I received new coordinates from a long-range galaxy transcender today. There's been a disturbance in the gravitational resonance synchronization between this sector and Earth. It's important that the ship leave as soon as possible to minimize transduction problems."

"What's causing it?" asked Nick with heightened concern.

"They either don't know or aren't saying," answered Matt. "I hope it's not more trouble. Anyway, I wanted to say goodbye to you both and to wish you the best for the future."

"Thank you, Matt," said Nick. "I'm sorry you won't be able to join us at the wedding. We will miss you very much."

"Yes, I'm sorry I won't be able to be there. Maybe I'll come back someday and see you and you're children. Wouldn't that be a surprise?"

"Matt, you'll always be welcome at our house," said Tara, giving him a parting hug.

The two partners stood facing each other for a moment, and then they hugged warmly, realizing that it might be the last time they would ever see each other.

That afternoon, Nick, Tara, Ruskin, Trila, Range, Dr. Gefert, Erik, Jon, and many of the townspeople went to the site of the space module to say goodbye to Matt. He enthusiastically mingled with the crowd and personally said farewell to them all. Then he stepped up into the spaceship and, from a window, waved back to them.

The ensuing blastoff was relatively quiet, and Nick raised his arm in salute as the ship gradually disappeared from sight. Tara looked into his eyes and could see a tear silently trickle down his cheek. She knew he had given up much to stay with her.

Chapter Eight

It was a simple church wedding with only relatives and close friends present. Vows were exchanged, and celebrant's words were poignant and terse:

"Love one another always, even in sickness, and raise children a credit to our community and to God."

The reception, by contrast, was exhilarating. It was held in a special reception hall where drinks and music flowed freely. Glittering arrays of candelabra lit the hall with a soft, intimate brightness, and the musicians plied their instruments with gusto and finesse. People sat at the tables or danced in the open area, as their mood inclined.

Tara was on the floor a lot as many younger as well as older men asked her to dance. She saved most of the slow ones for Nick, as he had learned the steps, and when she didn't, Trila and Tes often sought him for a partner. Tes was Range's wife, and a good friend of Tara's. Range and Ruskin and others made toasts in honor of the newly married couple. Nick and Tara sometimes kissed when dancing or at the table; it was expected, and whenever they did, the crowd signaled their delight by clapping. He asked her during a lull in the music how much longer the night would last.

"Not much longer for us," she mysteriously replied, looking into his eyes.

Sensing that there was more she wasn't saying, he tried to discern what it was and asked, "What is it? What happens next?"

Before she could reply, the music changed to a soft but upbeat melody of very distinctive style. The people on the floor stopped dancing, and everyone began clapping slowly in a cadenced tempo.

"It's time for us to leave," she spoke softly. "Just follow me."

Tara led the way with a graceful, swaying movement toward the back of the hall as Nick followed. Then she ascended a narrow staircase while the crowd whistled, cheered, and increased the tempo of their clapping.

At the top of the stairs, there was a little veranda, and from there Tara blew kisses to the guests and motioned Nick to do the same. The noise level of the crowd rose in response, and Tara turned to Nick and embraced him. Then she threw her head back and looked up at him with such tenderness that he bent down to kiss her, forgetting momentarily all the people beneath them. Tara slowly backed away from him and slipped out of his embrace. She turned to the crowd and waved, then pushed open the door behind them. She led him into the room and closed the door, shutting out much of the sounds from below. From behind the door they faintly heard the musicians change tempo again to a mellow serenade.

They stood there for a moment in darkness. Tara squeezed his hands and left him briefly to light two candles. In the soft light of the candles, Nick felt that Tara had never looked more beautiful. Her eyes sparkled, and he could see that there were tears in them. He asked if there was anything wrong. She told him that she was so happy. He embraced her tenderly, kissing her full lips softly. She melted into his arms and whispered something in his ear. He held her tight and they kissed, and for a time the universe stood still.

In the morning the sunlight that streamed into the room through the blinds found them lying side by side, arms entwined around each other. Tara awakened first, and for awhile she watched Nick sleep. When he opened his eyes, she snuggled closer. "I love you so much, my Earthman."

"I love you too, my darling."

"I wonder what our future will be like?" she thought out loud, raising her head.

"We'll find that out, together."

"Together," she echoed, drawing closer.

Beach Time for Two

She traveled with the man of her life,
through the years together,
the top rolled down,
enjoying the warm coastal breezes.

Florida, heading south on Tamiami Trail,
the sun setting behind them,
kingfishers swoop down for a catch,
on the reddening crest of the sea.

She said, "Let's go to the island,"
they turn, cross the bridge, and are there,
continuing along the ocean,
noting charming places to stay.

"Oh, Charles, let's turn in here,"
a chalet right on the sea,
soon, they are in their room,
stepping out the back door.

Holding hands they walk to the beach,
to watch the riot of red,
the sun sinks into the sea.
"Beautiful," she said, turning to him.

They walk along in the twilight,
slowly, arm in arm, bodies touching,
delighted at the fragrance of the ocean,
happy to be together.

They go back to their room,
through the quaint back door,
he turns on a light,
enough to play a favorite CD.

They dance to the music,
the lamp splashes their shadows,
onto the walls,
they hold each other tight.

She leaves him to light a candle,
and turns off the small lamp light,
she kisses, with heartfelt affection,
and he responds in kind.

Their dancing over,
they move closely with each other,
expressing endearments, tenderness,
touching, caressing, giving their love.

Love Strokes
245

They sleep in the big bed,
in darkness, except for the moon,
that spreads its dreamy silver,
through the blinds, onto white sheets.

They had traveled far together,
too long without repose,
this was the respite she wanted,
to sleep with him by the sea.

It was all that she had hoped for,
sunshine, bathing, and sand,
with the one she had shared so much with,
who was now, and for always, her man.

Tom Molnar

Used Life

She stood there in the grocery store,
selecting produce.
No one you would notice.
Doing one of the ordinary chores of life.

She straightened up,
pushing her cart to a different section,
walking straight, yet carefully.
A delicate flower.

She had known much life,
and now she was alone.
She had a certain pride.
It showed.

Fifty years ago or so,
She turned heads.
A beauty, full of life.
She gave it all away.

Love Strokes

For him, and their children.

Three sons, two daughters.

She smiled, secretly.

The memories came back.

Her husband,

the finest man she ever knew.

Not that they didn't fight.

But how they loved!

The children, and how they grew,

important people, some now.

The darling grandchildren,

The great grandchildren.

"Ma'am, are you Ok?

Can I help you find something?"

She returned to the now.

"No, thank you, son."

She continued on her way,
and came to the checkout counter.
No one you would notice.
Just an older lady.

Decision on High

I stood on a precipice,
And carefully looked at the valley far below.
The wind swirled about me,
making me afraid to go too close
to the edge.

Times had not been good.
I had been depressed.
There were rocks below.
I was fascinated by it all.

Easing nearer the edge,
I looked down,
and felt the glory,
as the whispering wind
caught at my clothing.

Tom Molnar

It had been a tough climb.
It was a good feeling,
sitting on the edge.
All power was in my hands,
to go or stay.

Slowly, I turned to reach back,
for a letter in my pocket.
Pulling it out, I reread it again.
It meant a lot to me.

It told me someone cared.
Maybe I was worth caring about.
A sigh, and I slowly moved back.
Not today, friend. Not today

Harvey and Emma

Harvey was an old black man,
Emma stayed by his side.
For many long years they had lived together.
Together, as man and wife.

Harvey said things were changing.
There was altogether too much strife.
He feared for them both, and bolted the doors.
They didn't go out at night.

"The neighborhood is bad," he said.
"The young folks is out of control."
"Too much drugs and drinkin'" said she.
What to do? They didn't know.

There was a time, a peaceful time,
they remembered from long ago,
when folks were nicer and kinder,
too bad, it was no longer so.

A different neighborhood might be better,
they thought from time to time,
but money was the crux of that,
they couldn't save a dime.

Her health was failing,
his was too,
they might not be around too long,
the truth of that they both knew.

But she really loved her Harvey,
and he really loved her so,
and they shared something together,
that made life beautiful.

To some, their love might seem common,
at a glance who would recognize?
Till you felt it in their presence,
and saw it in their eyes.

A love that was true and powerful,
a love that was tender with care,
the love of a man and a woman,
timeless, no matter when or where.

Love Strokes

This poem is different in that it's about lust, not love. It's included here because to me it's special.

Don Pablo And Chiquita

High up on the veranda, Don Pablo sits with an unknown friend,
Watching, as darkness slowly creeps over the land.

Down below, near the tiny stream,
Lovely Chiquita puts her little ones to bed,
In the narrow wooden hut that is her home.

Suddenly, laughter rings out over the savanna.
Don Pablo is amused by something his friend has said.
It is an evil, demented laughter that disturbs the evening quiet,
and poor Chiquita crosses herself and lights a candle to dispel the gloom.

A glance at the veranda shows nothing. All is dark.

And yet there is movement, as his friend knows.

Don Pablo is going out. Even now, in the darkness,

he is moving toward where the creek meets the swamp.

The heat is rabid tonight.

All the creatures, large and small feel it and sweat.

Insects rise in clouds,

and a man moves silently through the darkness.

Chiquita arranges her bolts of yarn for the morning.

She takes a last look at Pedro and Maria, breathing peacefully in their sleep.

She blows out the candle and removes her chemise,

before sinking into her low lying bed.

Love Strokes

There is a knocking at the door.

She calls out, "Who is it?"

"It is I, Don Pablo," he says with a smile.

"It is too late," she answers. "You cannot come in."

"I want something, Chiquita. You know what it is."

"No!" she replies. "Never!"

"Must I sever the bolt Chiquita? Is that what you want?"

"Leave me alone, Senor. You have your own woman."

Alert for his movement, she hears soft rasping sounds.

Silently, she edges to the kitchen,

where she finds her long slicing knife.

I am ready for you, Don Pablo.

Outside, the rasping sound stops.

Quietly, quietly, the door is slowly opened.

Chiquita crosses herself and prepares to meet her adversary.

Don Pablo steps into the room.

"Chiquita. Chiquita, I know you're in here."

He walks slowly toward where he knows she sleeps.

"Ahhh-eeee!" she cries as she plunges the blade deep into his back.

Don Pablo cries out and falls to the floor, clutching his chest.

"I am sorry," she tells him, wrenching the blade from his body.

Don Pablo turns over and looks up at her.

He tries to say something, but the words do not come.

He turns his head, his body quivers, and then all is still.

Love Strokes

Chiquita cries softly, her copious tears falling on Don Pablo.

She wakens her little ones, telling them they have to leave.

Quickly, she packs their few possessions into a bag,

then silently leads her children away, hoping to find a better life.

She's Still There

An old man squinted at the sun,
and silently asked, why so hot?
No answer came.
He trudged back to his dwelling.

A few stars came out that night.
He looked up at them,
and he thought about her.
So young, so beautiful,
the maiden who listened to his heart.

Ah, that was long ago.
He paused at the doorstep,
then turned to go inside.
He saw her asleep, in the chair.
Yes, she was still there,
The maiden who listened to his heart.

A Small Reunion

I loved her,
my heart was on fire.
I loved her,
with so much desire.

She came to me,
so much like a child.
I held her close,
so deeply inspired

The wedge set between us,
was broken in two.
Two hearts separated,
became one anew.

I held her far longer,
into the night.
She kissed me and told me,
"Let's never more fight."

Tom Molnar

I promised with fervor,
and kissed her again.
She smiled, before sleeping,
still holding my hand.

About The Author

Tom grew up in Indianapolis, joined the Army and saw the world while repairing electronic equipment. After getting his degree, he worked many years matching people with jobs. Married, with two sons and two daughters, he lives near Chicago and enjoys writing both romantic and adventure fiction. He recently became a proud, first time grandfather, of triplets.

Apple Valley Press
P.O. Box 635
St. John IN
46373

☐ **Love Strokes** (Including *Bridestar*) $14.00

Available at Amazon.com and some bookstores

Forthcoming

☐ ***Bridestar, Book II***

☐ ***Bridestar, Book III***

☐ ***Defending Her Fortress*** (A high adventure historical romance set in Italy after the fall of the Roman Empire)

Love Strokes

Notes:

Printed in the United States
39461LVS00003B/448-486